DEAF TO THE CITY

DEAF TO THE CITY

Marie-Claire Blais

TRANSLATED BY CAROL DUNLOP

THE OVERLOOK PRESS
WOODSTOCK   NEW YORK

First published in 1987 by
The Overlook Press
Lewis Hollow Road
Woodstock, New York 12498

Library of Congress Cataloging-in-Publication Data

Blais, Marie-Claire.
  Deaf to the city.

Translation of: Le sourd dans la ville.
I. Title.
[PQ3919.B6S613 1987]   843   86-43063
ISBN 0-87951-276-8 (cloth)
ISBN 0-87951-296-2 (paperback)

Printed in the U.S.A.

To J.R.

O Lord, grant each his own, his death indeed,
the dying which out of that same life evolves
in which he once had meaning, love, and need.

For what in dying so alienly shakes us
is that it's not our death, but one that takes us
only because we've not matured our own.

Rainer Maria Rilke
(*From the translation by
J.B. Leishman*)

EDITOR'S NOTE

Italicized phrases appeared in English in the original French text.

HE STOOD WATCHING THE BUSY TRAFFIC IN THE STREET from the window of the Hôtel des Voyageurs, wearing the apron he wore at lunchtime when he helped his mother in the restaurant, his face pinched in the sallow light, his restlessness frozen for a moment in meditation, so that suddenly he looked like the very countenance of pain captured by Munch in *The Scream*; and like that anonymous figure whose silent cry fills the painter's canvas, Mike rested his heavy head on his frail hands and with his wide-eyed questioning gaze, his pupils enlarged with concern, he challenged the world — or rather the various silhouettes that made up his world at that instant: the people passing by out on the street, his mother, the men she was waiting on at the bar, Tim the Irishman who was standing near him unfolding his newspaper, all the strangers going in and out of the hotel, each and every one of them — just when it seemed as though his quivering, half-open mouth was about to emit an endless scream to remind the indifferent human mass gathered there, crouching or musing over a glass, a sunbeam, or some other scant dose of morning pleasure, that even if it were not a shame to live as they were living, as tranquilly and inconsequentially as flies — although flies had been blessedly spared those human cravings that weigh down so many good and wicked men alike — even if this were not cause for shame, it was scandalous to live and die without ever managing to strip away the damning halo that branded their foreheads with the sentence: "You shall suffer on earth...." It was engraved on all things, Mike thought, even on old Tim's flabby face as he muttered in English, his nose in the paper, *Do you believe everything you read in the paper, Gloria, do you? Hé, the kid wants to go to the movies, hé, a blue movie, Mike, what's the matter with him, Gloria, anyway? They all took their money out, they're crazy....* " Day after day the same sounds came stumbling from the wrinkled, bitter mouth: *"What a bastard he is, hé, what a bastard, take care of your heart, my Gloria, take care of your heart..."* and Gloria responded to the fetid murmur of the bar with a haughty, ferocious sensuality that would have struck them dead in a single glance if her body had been as taut with hatred as her soul, but her body was bored and it gave in, gave in with the softness of her handsome, languorous arms and the curve of the placid, voluptuous breast she offered up to all, it yielded despite herself to the torpor, to the somehow unclean fondling of so many fingers, "and that's O.K.," thought Mike, "just so long as she doesn't start pawing them all over and getting them excited... if it rains Tim will take me to a dirty movie... three orders of spaghetti in the oven, yes, just so long as Mom's hand doesn't slide any lower...." Lethargy, the first caress of the day, Gloria thought, "If you don't like it you don't have to look, Mickey, don't forget your father wasn't just anybody, he was the great Luigi, we'll go to the hospital for your treatment and then we'll take in all the movies you want, *stop it, Tim, you could kiss my royal ass, O.K.?* Why don't you go fetch me the porno slicks at the corner, na, not for the kid, for me, he don't read much, that one, his head hurts too much. . . . " "How'd it all start?" asked Tim, his lips slobbering against Gloria's face, *"there's always a beginning, hé, always a beginning. . . . "* "It's nothing!" Gloria snapped back, "nothing at all, he's O.K., they got rid of his tumour, going to take him all the way to San Francisco on my bike this summer, *shit*, won't it be a pleasure not to see your holy mug, you damned Irishman!" "Well, what if his father turned out to be just an ordinary Italian," said Tim, *"or just me, your old lover, just an ass like me, hé?"* "You holding that spaghetti up for Easter, Mike? Get a move on, and wash some cups for coffee while you're at it, what're you standing there like that for with your tongue hanging out?" Mike, with an anguished look, avoided his mother's glance and hid his head in his arm. "It's nothing, Mom, nothing. I feel hot." "The doctor told you it's normal to feel hot, that spaghetti's going to be burned to a crisp. . . . " It was a cool day, the street bright with sunshine, and before long the student who ran down from the mountain each day would break into the street then the park with his long-limbed weightless flight, and in a moment Mike would be left only with a sense of the perfection of the runner's muscular life, the spirited body dashing forward towards life itself, he would be no more than a long back stiffened by effort and the tight clothes binding it, a scarlet blob about to disappear around the corner, "Tell me now,

Tim, what d'ya know about the role of sex in life? Nothing, I bet, nothing, cause it's up to us women to know about those things.... As for me, I'm a mother, first and foremost a woman and a mother, and mistress all around, or lover if you prefer, *my old boy*.... " The Irishman's big fist was resting on Gloria's chest, the runner was coming down the mountain, still coming down, and he must get a bit winded, Mike thought, the whole city was running out of breath bit by bit, noise and light dilating it, the aroma of coffee was invading the dimly lit kitchen and Mike said to Lucia who was staring at the burned spaghetti, "Hurry up and take care of Jojo and we'll go out, it's a nice day, we can take a walk in the park...." "I don't want to be late for school," Lucia replied. "I'm afraid I'll miss my bus. Why don't you feed her yourself?" "I don't know how," Mike answered. "Just put the spoon in her mouth, see, like this — Mom feeds you stuff that's nothing but juice when you can't swallow! D'you know who her father is, Mike?" Lucia's tiny shadow went bouncing through the yard and disappeared. "Eat up now," Mike said to Jojo, "then we'll go out in the sun... " but Jojo refused the spoon Mike tried to slip into her mouth, she was laughing and crying at the same time and then all of a sudden a question seemed to fix itself in her black, uncannily knowing eyes. "Do *you* know why I was born," she seemed to ask Mike, "what I'm doing here?" Mike went on feeding her patiently with the kind of dreamy, slightly far-off gentleness that had come over his movements in the past few months. "Let's go play in the park, Jojo... but stay away from the horses, sometimes they get mad if you bother them," the grass was coming up in the park, it was spring, "This summer we'll go to San Francisco," said Mike as he set the child down in a patch of light and warmth, and Jojo immediately began to run every which way with Mike running after her, laughing, laughing because it was nice out at long last and in winter you couldn't see or hear anything when the snow and the wind blinded you, and now, as he went skipping along in the path of his sister's fragile destiny, Mike listened to his heart beating in his chest, "Where I'll be next year, maybe I won't hear it any more." Jojo was laughing, falling down and scrambling to her feet, thinking to scare Mike by hiding behind trees. Mike let her whirl about him, stronger for the kind of glow he felt in her presence, as if not even the mighty, unsightly cathedral that dominated the city could protect the child as he could just by letting the back of his hand brush over her hair, this was life, this was living and the people walking and scurrying around him didn't know it, none of the people spilling out of the subway in groups or emerging from the station and the banks knew it — or were their hearts making as much noise as the torrent that seemed to roar through his veins, yes, perhaps. . . . It was a bright day but Gloria had forgotten about the electric sign, and the red letters sparkled with their nocturnal fire: *Come as you are, day and night, chez Luigi.* Tim would come staggering out of the hotel, others would stop in for a beer or a coffee, Gloria had a man in the house but he was bad, Mike thought, she also had dogs to protect her and they were bad too, "but it's better than being alone," he reflected, and the sky was so blue you saw it a lot closer, without fear. "Look, Jojo, the birds are back . . ." but the small ball of life wouldn't nestle long in Mike's hands, it drew close only to run off immediately, far away, already far away, leaving in its place a waft of perfume, a breath, now it was just a curly head of hair, curly like Gloria's, a big head for a child, thought Mike, a head set atop a bundle of woollen clothes since Gloria hadn't noticed that spring had arrived, and inside this coloured package there was life, life that knew how to walk and run unaided towards a goal that didn't yet seem at all obscure although it would cloud over eventually, maybe even the very next day. The runner, Mike thought, must have turned the corner a long time ago, as if sucked up into the blue sky, for it was already time for the girl — he didn't know her, but he had become used to seeing her — to come down the mountain for a cup of coffee, to sit at the bar while Gloria hissed, mocking and impious, in her ear, "Say, love, what's your name again? Judith Langenais. . . . That's right, you told me yesterday, Judith Lange, Judith the Angel, you'll wake up in the gutter one day all the same, the cappuccino's on the house today cause it does me good to see you, it's a welcome change from Tim, you're a professor, hé, must be tough going sometimes what with the brats you got in schools today. . . . What d'you teach? Philosophy! Well, then, you ought to be able to answer my question: what's the role of sex in life?" Leaning against a tree while Jojo toyed with some pebbles at his feet, Mike observed the woman, his mother, from a distance, he was steeped in her, in her shamelessness, in her charitable lewdness, he didn't hate her, he respected her, even loved her sometimes, especially when the weather was nice and you had the illusion of suddenly seeing her face and the eager movements of her features very close up, when the words she pronounced every day resounded in your ears as if they were rising from her entrails, a stream of lewdness that was also Gloria, that was Gloria and nobody else, for it wasn't just any woman who was willing to be called Gloria and to have had a husband murdered in the street, and a bar that might also become a bloody stage from one night to the next, what kind of a life was it after all, being called Gloria and having dyed hair and a sick child, "and others who aren't doing so bad but that's just it, you've got to feed them, all the same the best part of the T-bone's for my dogs in case we're attacked one day, you understand, love? You still haven't answered the sex question, should be a cinch for you, being into that philosophy stuff you should know all about it!" Judith didn't answer, Mike knew Judith never answered Gloria's questions, he had seen her coming down from the street's golden summit, Judith, Judith Lange, the Angel, as his mother called her, although nothing about her made you think of an angel, she walked with her books under her arm, she had a class at two, she taught philosophy, her shiny raincoat was open at the collar and a gold chain glittered on her bare neck, a rather buxom girl, that was how Mike saw her approaching in the distance, first recognizing her head, then her neck that she never covered, not even in winter, and he recalled that when spring came she suddenly seemed lighter, slimmer, as if everything floated around her, maybe it was just the shiver of the air, unlike the runner who flew along with the current of the buildings, of the houses, Judith Lange drew near with a slow, heavy step, her feet sank into the ground and then she came back up towards you, maybe it was her slowness and the invisible weight of her gait, stealthy as a cat's, that stirred the air, she said nothing when Gloria asked her an indiscreet question, only smiled, yet Gloria thought she heard her say, "But Gloria, sex is everything, life, death, everything, Gloria." But she never said anything, Mike thought, it was the kindness of her smile that traced on her lips the words Gloria alone could really understand, then Gloria, appeased, would say, "Love, you wouldn't think, seeing me like this behind my cash register, that I had an ancestor who came from Norway like me, she was the first woman doctor received by the Academy....And even me, Gloria, my eldest daughter Berthe is studying for the bar, not the alcoholic kind, mind you, no, she's in law school, it's a change for us but the girl's got a heart of stone, won't have anything to do with us, even disowns her father! But I've still got my Mike, my Michel, and I swear you'll see us take off on the bike for San Francisco this summer! They won't keep him at the hospital, he's my little boy after all. You've got time yet, have another coffee, at your age I was always shacked up with one guy or another, didn't give a damn about school, you see I've had sex on my mind for a pretty long time now...." But maybe Judith Lange wouldn't be coming today. Gloria said Mike pretended to be deaf when she spoke, deaf to her groans of pleasure, to the wrenching sighs of her revolt, deaf to everything, she said, and yet he heard her when she spoke of "life, sex, and death", and again of "sex, death, and life", those words that churned about freely in Gloria's mind and perhaps hers was the only mind in the world that harboured them, thought Mike who wanted to be like Gloria, working late into the night, sometimes seeking out her clients in funeral parlours, she would tell Judith about that too some day, sex was Gloria's legend, she would tell it all to Judith one day, but Jojo was living her own life under the tree, the tree Mike was caressing, his palms moist, you could tell when you leaned against it that it was a tree that still had many years of life ahead, Mike thought, yes, the day would come, tonight or tomorrow, it might be fiercely violent or sweetly murderous, the soul just took off, all the souls of the dead were wandering in the sun, looking for someone to understand, someone who would let them into his or her thoughts, even Gloria's thoughts about sex, life, and death, one day Mike would understand everything, everything that was dormant in Gloria, on Judith's lips, the delivered soul went elsewhere, went to all those places to which it had been denied admittance during its joyous but often terrible captivity, and it might be only a short time before Mike's soul also knew that flight, that dance deep within the hearts that were now closed to him. Mike, still leaning against the tree, suddenly forgot about Judith as he noticed three boys in the park lying in the sun, spread out on a bed of grass that seemed to have been made for them at that instant; Jojo had probably run around them, chirping, but the boys, dozing, remained aloof in their wholesome nonchalance, each of them resting his head on the other's leg, and in the moment of unexpected languor in which sleep had caught them off guard, in such a rigid, three-sided pose that one might have taken them for statues, thought Mike, the only thing that still recalled their existence or the fact that they had been alive ten minutes earlier — and they had been, they'd spoken loudly, they'd quarrelled — was a pair of running shoes;

one of the shoes that no longer served to walk and run had been separated from its twin, and during the battle that had brought the three boys together the shoe, harassed, molested at the hands of the enemy, tossed up like a ball, had landed close to the tree and Mike, and if in the distance the flash of blue and yellow T-shirts added a bright touch to the triangular tomb the boys seemed to form, only the battered, saddened shoe appeared, as Mike contemplated it, to claim an existence proper; broken, subjugated by its owner, it knew, better than Mike, the boy it had shod and protected against the cold, it had soaked up the sweat of his joys and his sufferings, it had loved, cried, laughed, and suddenly it was just an obsolete thing that would soon be cast aside for another and it lay there, close to Mike who watched it living its final moments of revolt in the sun. Eternal Gloria, celestial Gloria, thought Gloria of herself, she gave all men their bottle, there could be no higher philosophy than the one Gloria dispensed to all, her body's fluids drenching the arid earth where everything one loved would die tomorrow; it was Friday, Judith was having lunch at her parents' house, Madame Langenais was asking her daughter what she was going to do later on, she was an attentive mother and Judith had every reason to be proud of her, Marianne, Gisèle, and Micheline were wearing their school uniforms "but they're not severe enough," Madame Langenais informed her husband, "the skirts are too short this year..." and she hardly dared let her gaze slide over her daughters' splendid thighs — the stockings stopped below the knees and all the rest was on display, the healthy, silken flesh and the pleats of the navy blue skirt not quite covering it, Marianne, Gisèle, and Micheline would go off to play tennis this afternoon as usual rather than study, and of course, Madame Langenais explained to her husband, their studies took a back seat to everything else, and Judith asked her father if he had been afraid before performing that morning's operation, no, he hadn't been afraid, "strangely," he told Judith, it was afterwards that fear really gripped him, "even when the operation has been successful," the soup was served, and Madame Langenais suddenly wondered, as if it were a fact she had never noticed until this particular Friday, why her daughter had green eyes when nobody else in the family had green eyes, teaching philosophy, it was no career for a woman, what would become of her later on, good God, she had surgeon's hands like her father, she would rather not know what Judith did with her hands, hands so firm yet delicate, there was no way of knowing anything about Judith since she no longer lived at home, as for Marianne, Gisèle, and Micheline one knew just about all there was to know, Madame Langenais still decided what books they read, or practically, but Judith's soul eluded her completely and for a mother there was something obscure in that, an irritating, wilful secrecy, then they had finished eating, and Gisèle and Micheline could be heard laughing and trying to find their tennis rackets "in their mess of a room," remarked Madame Langenais while Judith silently ground a piece of fruit between her small, cat-like teeth, and Marianne, her mother realized, had just sat down on her father's lap, her knees red and so bare, so bare, thought Madame Langenais, anyway she was too big to sit on her father's knees now, at her age, thought Madame

Langenais, wondering at the same time about the gardener, she'd have to look after that, Judith had asked why Gilbert didn't eat with them and Madame Langenais had firmly replied, "Gilbert prefers eating alone in the kitchen," that was the way things were, she wasn't going to give in to Judith's whims, to that Communist, she mused, staring at her with her round eyes, Judith, she had to keep reminding herself that this was her flesh, her blood, Marianne was addressing her father, "You don't know anything, Papa, no, you don't know anything, you told me you knew everything but you don't know anything at all," her father explained that mathematics had changed a lot since his youth but Marianne wasn't listening and Madame Langenais, while carefully watching her family, was casting furtive glances towards the garden where Gilbert was coming and going with a shovel, the tip of his cap just visible beneath the window, social classes no longer existed, a shame, was there a place left on earth where people still respected them, of course everybody had a right to his or her political ideas, but how did Judith spend her nights, the word "night" sprang up like a sudden menace in Madame Langenais' mind, the word was the very essence of insubordination, night, sumptuous night, secret night, no, better to ignore what Judith did at night, the word was so heavy with sighs, with abandonment, and these easy-going girls thought their parents had ceased loving each other, but the night, the night, and all of a sudden Judith had risen and wound her giant arms around her mother's shoulders and Madame Langenais had heard the hissing of her raucous voice in her ear, a voice that was saying, insidious, loving, "Maman, dear

Maman, Josephine, I love you in spite of everything...."
Madame Langenais, accustomed to her daughter's affectionate outbursts, hadn't budged, the tip of Gilbert's cap
could still be seen bobbing up and down beneath the
window as he passed, and Madame Langenais was over-
come by a kind of sinner's sadness, she realized she'd been
lacking in charity, Judith's warm breath against her cheek
evoked the latent fault, the fault that was so ancient,
irreparable, a habit already, it was too late, even if Judith
was a Communist, she had no proof of that but where
Judith was concerned it was fitting to imagine the worst,
she thought, it was already too late to ask Gilbert in to
share the family's meals, Madame Langenais had no reason
to complain, didn't she have affectionate, maybe over-
affectionate daughters — Marianne was still cuddling up
against her father — yes, but how did Judith spend her
nights, and Gilbert kept passing back and forth with his
shovel, his piles of earth, we'll have beautiful roses this
year, Josephine, I love you in spite of everything, the "in
spite of everything" ringing in Madame Langenais' ear,
there was a rebuke in it or at least a hint of rebuke,
Madame Langenais pushed her daughter off gently, saying,
"I've already told you I don't want you calling me by my
name...not in this house...ask your father if I'm not
right..." and suddenly, while Judith's arms were still
resting on her neck, Madame Langenais remembered a
young couple she had noticed that morning on her way to
the bank, they had been waiting at a street corner and
looking each other over they had on an amorous impulse
brusquely grasped each other in a long embrace, passion-
ately intertwined right there on the sidewalk where they

stood, Marianne's bare knees flashing before her were suddenly confused with the enchanting yet dangerously sensual explosion of the two young people in their coloured shorts, each giving the other, without any particular reason, this entangling of knees and tongues, drowning in broad daylight, they had yielded to the moment without shame or reproach, each so lost in the other as long as the hypnotic embrace lasted that Madame Langenais had felt herself a witness to their bodies' most intimate movements beneath the transparent, multicoloured shorts that offered such scant protection on such a cool morning. Suddenly Judith was no longer there, Madame Langenais was alone in the empty house with its blue drapes, from the garden, on the mountainside, you could see the whole city, where was Judith now, what was she doing, a class at two, Madame Langenais was going to go out and offer Gilbert a bit of advice, red roses or white roses, Judith's breath was hot, before long the whole city would be in blossom, fragrant, so fragrant, and Mike had dozed off vaguely while his sister played at his feet, he was still standing against the tree — "Don't put that poison in your mouth, Jojo..." — old Tim came out of the drugstore with his porno papers under his arm, his old dog trailing after on a rope, Tim and the dog staggering towards their bench under the brotherly hundred-year-old tree that awaited them, the tree, the bench, these were their shores and neither Tim nor his dog noticed Mike, flotsam in the sun, they went on, kept going, they didn't fall, they were walking almost straight, the entire city was feverish with men and sounds but they were still headed for their bench, the old dog was also called Tim and he too was Irish, you could no longer tell which of the two was at the end of the rope, the one with the logger's jacket or the one with tattered fur and unsteady gait, both were hungry but once at the bench they would share the crumbs of the same sandwich, they would watch the women together, their desires coming through in identical fashion, two muzzles dripping with drool, old Tim and his old dog, they were close to Mike now, running out of breath together, but they didn't see him leaning shakily against a tree, you couldn't really buckle under with pain or sadness, you could only give in, give in slightly on such a good day, weighed down by that something, maybe it was ecstasy, the ecstasy of being alive, and suddenly the vision of his mother came back to Mike in the whirl of old Tim and his dog, of the plaid jacket and the haggard dog at the end of the rope, flotsam in the sun, but they were still on their feet and so was he, slackening a tiny bit as he leaned against the tree, the tree that would always be there, tomorrow or later, in rain or snow, Mike saw again his mother, saw old Tim pinching her hip that morning, slipping his shifty hands into Gloria's armpits, so old Tim didn't know that at night Gloria was transformed, that she became for her son something terribly severe, the image of crucifixion, the Mother of Sorrow, that was Gloria, she had a man or several men with her in her room, they were all bad like the five police dogs in the yard, that night she was sleeping with Charlie, "My goddamned hooligan on probation, you don't even know how to make love," she shouted, "leave the door open in case my kid calls me...." "What did Charlie do, Mom?" "Nothing much, he killed someone one day, he was too young, he doesn't even remember...." Charlie had killed, maybe he would kill again that very night, Lucia, Jojo, and Luigi 2 were downstairs, all the people Gloria knew had killed, but it was time to sleep, nothing had been written on sleep, not yet, and sleep, white as a snow field, was calling Mike, come, come, and Mike would not be slow to obey, love and sleep also belonged to those who had killed, Gloria and Charlie would soon sleep just like everybody else, "All the same, leave a light on in the hall, just in case he calls me, first time I've ever heard of a guy getting homesick for prison, never saw the likes of it!" Sleep was still as pure as a sheet of blank paper but in the feeble light coming from the hall it seemed as though an unknown, detached hand had come to write on it, yes, a hand was writing by itself, drawing on the wall, the design was imperceptible, the work of an ant, the written expression of the terror that crept along the wall, something was pursuing Mike, hunting him down even when he hid under the sheets, or maybe the devastating parasite was lodged in his own body and it was nothing but his own shadow that he saw on the wall, it was his head, his thronging head that had become a refuge for these larvae; and his heart that usually throbbed so wildly, pounding with fever, was suddenly beating noiselessly, without echo, maybe it wasn't a parasite after all but that formidable She, maybe the Unnameable had just entered his body, and surely this deaf heart, this voiceless heart was no longer his own; and yet, though he heard no sound rising to his lips, his moan too low to be perceptible, it was she after all, Gloria, who now bent heavily over his iron bed, she, Mother of all Sorrow, of the crucified, "Stop screaming, come on, I'm right here..." and cradled him in her breasts, he had watched it all flee, even the ghost of his terror, the hand writing by itself on the wall, the worm of his own destruction nestling into the purity of the night, and his heart had taken up its own rhythm and song once again, "But why do you give your mother such frights?" Not even old Tim who was so proud of being a Catholic knew that the saints were no longer in heaven but among us on earth, in the lightning flash of our pains, he was stretched out on the bench with the panting dog, still holding on to the end of the rope although there was no need to hold the old dog who had been Tim's master for such a long time now, old Tim saw the sky through clouds of alcohol, it wasn't a sky full of angels furious because he'd had too much to drink, it wasn't a sky so blue that it was like blue lake-water passing over his eyes pained by visions, no, it was the sea, his own country's sea, he only had to dream a bit and he found it again, a pale sea waiting for him on the other side of a pine-covered mountain, then it slipped out of sight and came back again with a tumultuous clamour, his native sea that had thrown him up here on this bench with an aging dog for company, he no longer knew how many years had passed, if he let the dream continue the bench became soft dunes under his back while the sea moved by with perfect, rigid tranquillity, a woman was coming down towards him, Gloria, the woman who had been the village schoolteacher during his childhood in the suburbs of Limerick, a nun hiking up her skirt and leaping over boulders — old Tim's dog had sneezed and the spell was broken, old Tim was back on the bench and would have to wait until tomorrow to find his native sea again, he grumbled, grumbled, *"Those bastards,*

those bastards," moaning when a boisterous gang of adolescents, trampling the new grass with an insolent, dancing
tread, began to bark just for a laugh, "woof woof," tossing
the "woof woof" to old Tim and his dog more as a mock
homage than as an insult; it so stung the drunkard's
delicate soul that he spit with scorn but they went on
barking, "Hi, woof woof," and old Tim began to dream, he
was gunning them all down with his rifle, it didn't matter
if his hand was a bit shaky and he had no rifle, only Tim's
old dog was touched by the music and suddenly light-
hearted under his tattered coat he perked up his nose and
ears and answered with drawn-out echoes the amused
barks which, just this once, had been aimed at him, one
had so few laughs with old Tim, they would wind up in the
city pound or the poorhouse sooner or later, yes, better
enjoy it while it lasted, *"Will you shut up, you monster!"* said
the Irishman, kicking his best friend, *"You bastard, I'll kill
you!"* and the dog, surprised, sad again, thought that, yes,
the city pound or the poorhouse, that was their future, but
old Tim had had too much to drink, he was "stiff to the
very roots", as Gloria put it, better stop barking, quiet
down, submit, since old Tim still held the end of the rope.
"All the same, some have it easy, sweet Jesus," muttered
Tim, noticing a taxi driver who was taking a nap in his car,
"just look at that bastard!" He was a thin man and seen in
profile he looked like a corpse, as though the solemn
stiffness of rigor mortis had allowed him to relax and listen
to the call coming in over the radio without slouching in
his seat: *"This is an emergency test only, an emergency test, when
you hear this sound, . . . "* then he'd fallen asleep and Tim saw
him thus from a distance, with his corpse's profile and the

nervous line of a last little smile that persisted, flouting Tim and his dog, the taxi driver telling Tim, *"Look how lucky I am, you, dog!"* Two images lingered still between the taxi driver's eyelashes, one of a Spanish star — at any rate that was how he imagined her — wiggling her hips on the street corner while waiting for a man, followed by the apparition of a Greek pope, or a person who bore a striking resemblance to a Greek pope with his black tunic and purple bonnet, accompanied by a businessman, nobody knew where they were all going like that, the mysterious convoy of the street coming and going, it didn't matter, thought the taxi driver, it was time for his nap, the rest of the world was thrashing about in vain in a swamp full of footsteps and sounds; perhaps it was at that very moment that Judith Lange, who was explaining Descartes to her students, suddenly noticed in the college yard, which was otherwise bare and ugly, a lone branch of white lilac trembling at the window, hovering alone as if the wind had blown it off the bush; it was probably an illusion, the yard was ugly and bare, but someone had nevertheless thought to plant the white lilacs that lined the wall, it was Judith who had been blind to their presence for so long, and suddenly the lilacs were alive again in the warm spring sun and the uncertain wind that carried a foreboding of summer gales and storms parted the branches of lilacs, their white intoxication floating in to Judith's nostrils, so sweet that she put her book aside — it was daylight, a radiant day bathing the students in the classroom and Judith herself in its generous, fragrant light, and silence had hushed the din of life, yet Judith thought of night, of nights full of love and all those fragrances and that light too, but night was when one was apt to give in to despair, "And what did you do last night?" her mother had asked, she had been to see Florence, she was the visitor who broke into lonely nights, but her students to whom she went on explaining Descartes knew nothing about that side of her life, who was this Florence after all?—a woman she'd met in a train station, a deserted eighteenth-floor apartment in a big city, Florence, a woman alone, where was her husband, where was her son, both dissolved in an ocean of memories. "No, you must not die," Judith had told her, and now the lilac branch seemed to confirm her statement which was suddenly truer than ever, the lilac branch whipped the window-pane, the sun flooded the classroom, springtime, spring, and summer before long, and Florence had not forsaken the joys of life, not yet, not that night, but now it was day again and a dull light fell on her furniture, on the pictures of her husband, of her son, her ruptured past frozen on the wall, Judith, a stranger, who was she after all, perhaps nothing more than a dream with which she'd consoled herself, the apartment was deserted once again, inhabited by so many bourgeois victories, Judith had said, maybe she was an anarchist, a revolutionary, inhabited, yes, by treasures, by china, but it was a distressing place since Florence had thought about dying there, Judith Lange, friend of suicides, sister of the inert martyrs of existence, where was she now, Florence wondered, why had she come to save her, for one night, for a few hours, when the fatal act was already stamped on her being, tonight or tomorrow, what was the sense of hanging on, respecting life when she was bound to it by nothing more than a young woman's smile illuminating the night, the apartment was deserted once again, Judith Lange was no longer there, the same nauseating sense of life rose in Florence's breast, and perhaps in thousands of other breasts at that very moment the same sensation was working its way into thousands of gloomy, silent hearts in spite of the glorious light that flooded the white lilacs in the college yard, into hearts that had already settled into silence as they advanced in their own solitary company towards that eternity of silence of which we know nothing; Florence was already dead, she thought as she cast an indifferent glance at her hands resting on her knees, dead hands resting on icy knees, Judith Lange had tried to warm them between her own but they were no longer fit for the reasonable task of living, how sweet it must be to belong to the community of the living, to love and live as they lived, deliciously and weightlessly; dying was a malady that weighed you down so, it was so heavy that even two frail hands on your knees felt like lead, and wasn't the painful light pouring from the sky spilling all over you and your paleness only to strike you down? This heavy heart was dead, and yet it kept on beating loudly in Florence's chest, it was a knell, a strident wail that nobody heard and it kept repeating, "Soon everything will be all over!" but time was passing and nothing was over yet, time was passing even more heavily today than yesterday, it passed with the sudden lulls and flashes of recovery that come to the condemned: that was when Judith's magnetic smile held the night hour at a distance, but the people of death remained close by, they were all gathered just beyond the fragile door, pressing against each other in these attics of time and silence: it was the city of the dead, the great faceless refuge, and if there was also a human presence lithely calling her back to life with warm breath and smiles, it was only Judith, a passer-by of whom Florence knew nothing except that she might never come back; and Judith at that moment noticed a couple of students walking under the canopy of white lilacs, they looked like an ordinary boy and girl, perhaps their only asset was the awkward charm of youth as they walked along close to each other, their hands barely touching, and Judith read in their features the desire of love, or love about to blossom even if they themselves were still all shyness and disorder; it was as though the brightness of the white lilacs, the radiant headiness that filled the air had caught them off guard in this uneasy enchantment without their quite realizing it; maybe they were holding their breath, maybe their pulses were slowing down as their eyes searched the other's and yes, perhaps it would take no more than the wind shivering among the lilacs, this barely perceptible movement of nature, to unite the boy and the girl who were still separated by the trembling shyness of their desires, which seemed as impenetrable as a wall as they stole cautious glances at each other; perhaps the slightest breath would suffice and they would find themselves uniting in each other everything which at that moment cut them off from all the rest, Judith would see them embrace during that moment of peace, the luminous veil would close in over them as the veil of death would close in over Florence tonight or tomorrow; but they were shy, the boy made an awkward move that brusquely detached him from his companion and then they disappeared as they had appeared, gentle and magic, and Judith took up her book again, Descartes, Descartes, but they weren't listening, they were all staring at the lilac branch at the window and Judith's body panted with the simple joy of being alive, she felt their gaze, their impatient caresses all around her, life was the only sacred philosophy — the words were still ringing in Florence's ears but she was on her own from now on, her sad face and the memory of her hands on her knees lingered still in Judith's soul, at long last she was going to go away she had told Judith, one can always die a bit farther on, in another city or in a hotel room, while preserving in one's home the still tepid appearance of everyday life, the car parked at the door, the light burning in the bathroom, those who passed by would think you were still caught up in life's traps, and the track left by all the gestures accomplished day after day — open a door, close it, read a book, put a glass away — this trail of gestures and objects would linger a long time after you had gone, haunting those who survived your absence, Judith Lange, friend of suicides, but you could not bypass the road to your own death, it was lurking in some sinister place, beneath a sinister light, preparations for the dull, fetid ceremony were already under way and it was close by, so close by; the person to be condemned walked listlessly or hurried along towards his place of execution, towards his livid shroud, and there were thousands of people like Florence shuffling across the face of the earth, coming and going at death's threshold, all stunned by a bruising, incomprehensible adversity; the arrows of misfortune never missed their mark and each victim wandered, wandered like Florence, stumbling again and again into the walls of the city, and all that could be seen of

Florence was the grey speck of her body against the vast, grey sky, and the heavy suitcase she was carrying that dragged her entire being down, down towards the bottomless pit of the world, it was a bright green suitcase which seemed huge compared to the woman carrying it, and Florence had filled it with old letters as if the weight of words written and delivered during a lifetime could help her take her leave and enter the earth again; in the meantime she wandered among the other travellers, dragging with her the enormously heavy suitcase that perhaps contained nothing more than ashes, and like the others she stumbled against the walls of the city, her soul exhausted and drained; sometimes she stopped walking and sat on a bench — she shared a yellow bench with another woman, a woman silent like herself, but the other woman wasn't going anywhere, her destiny was to wait for a train that would get her safely home to her family and her own kind by evening; Florence had envied the unknown woman, had even envied the woollen folds of her coat, for beneath the coat, beneath the leather gloves and the small handbag there was a woman, a living woman and her world, instead of the stray, dispossessed spirit, instead of the anguish that had become Florence's world ever since she left her apartment and her memories, and yet everyone would think she was still there, the light burning in the bathroom, the car at the door, still back there, yes, and she wandered, wandered, perhaps her soul had already left her body, she thought, yes, perhaps that was it, the almost weightless feeling she had beside this burden, can one possibly get lost in a city while dragging around such a weight, a heavy green suitcase pulling you towards the ground while all around there's nothing but vast, grey silence, while at the other end of a bench there's a silent woman who doesn't hear your breath, your lamentation, your cry, for she'll soon be home among her own, and the trains, their whistles and wails, trains coming in, going out, for the first time Florence noticed all the other people she had barely had a glimpse of through the screen at her window, suddenly they were all there, they existed, some- one had said, "Nice day today, isn't it?" and Florence observed, stupefied, the silent form that was no longer there, the woollen coat, the leather gloves, the small handbag, none of it existed now, the other end of the bench was suddenly occupied by a girl wrapped in misery, an extremely poor girl smelling of wine, and Florence was confronted with the filthy apparition of two bare legs that had been cold all winter; from her screened window, from her apartment that was so near the sky, Florence had never seen legs that had been cold during an entire winter this close up, the legs were still young, the socks and the boots that protected the benumbed feet had the look of wear, the transparency of old rags, but the creature abandoned there on the bench, who seemed to breathe the very breath of abandonment, was courageously saying to Florence, "Nice day today, isn't it?" Florence didn't answer as she contemplated the face and the legs that had endured the stigmata of bitter cold; injustice and evil were everywhere on earth, go away, leave it all behind, and the girl who had been cold all winter was saying, "On nice days like today I sure feel like taking off on a trip, but no money, no trip...." Florence didn't answer; she was accustomed to silence, one didn't speak to other people, they were there but one didn't speak to them, the sensation of fear only grew worse at their contact, and suddenly an old man who also seemed to have come in from a wintry, nocturnal path appeared in the light, he looked as though he were walking but he was in fact jogging on the spot, no, he wasn't walking, he moved his feet slowly, guided by his blind man's cane; the feet, the man, old age followed the cane but he didn't move, or barely, he must have come a long way, thought Florence, like the poor girl who had been cold all winter, maybe he was a man who thought about nothing, who had a hard time just existing, sweat running down his spine, his cane guiding him, blind, blind, like any object that moves us to pity he wandered blindly, adrift in the world and seeing nobody, neither Florence sitting on the bench nor the other woman; his blind memory held fast to the crude forces that had been crushing him for such a long time, cold, hunger, misery, it all moved along slowly with him and, like Florence, he could find no refuge anywhere, like Florence he was bitter, bitter, sapped, and blind, and he scorned the brutal forces that had debased the dignified man in him, of whom there wasn't a trace left, nobody even vaguely remembered him, that was what living was, when men were slain before their time only their ghosts remained and Florence thought, "Why doesn't he fall, he hasn't an ounce of strength left to continue," but like a worm the old man clung stubbornly to the surface of the earth and Florence felt fear stirring in her, it was all part of the same thing, her fear, his stubbornness, what's the use, what's the use — if this particular fear was intolerable it was because it carried other familiar sensations in its wake, and yet Florence, her heavy suitcase at her feet, remained calm, staring at the ridiculous hands resting on her knees, they were all alive, all of them, they were going to go home, eat, love, sleep, and she stayed on, the fear in her cutting her off from everything, even from their habits, and yet she remembered, yes, it was a familiar sensation, maybe one felt it even in the company of the powerful of this world, when she was with her husband for example, who was an influential man, a physicist, people respected him, the sensation of fear floated all around him, even if it was something invisible it was there lurking behind the malicious, enchanting screen of pleasure, everywhere, fear beneath the pure, tranquil sky, he was powerful, bent over sheets of paper lined with frigid figures and saying, "You're afraid, darling, but what are you afraid of?" When she moved it all moved with her, an immense, terrible chaos and dread and he knew nothing of it, he went on writing, meditating, sipping his cognac, they travelled first class, they were somewhere over Africa, alone, agitation seizing her high above the black abyss, and what would become of him now, she had no idea, the old man was still pushing his cane along before him, he had taken a few steps, with great difficulty but he had taken a few steps, and this filled Florence with a feeling of oppression, she had no idea how much longer it could go on this way, the old man with the cane, the girl who had been cold all winter, each of them passing before Florence like a sublime figure of her own life's throes, both of them, like herself, had fallen into the life-trap and were now struggling, frenetic and humiliated, with the duties imposed at birth, the obligation to enjoy life or suffer; they all had the impression they were wandering, advancing, but each of them was bound up in his own torment like Florence sitting on her bench and there could be nothing more terrifying than just being there, motionless against the grey immensity of the sky, being nothing more than that, Florence, a shapeless human being imprisoned by the evil forces of life, and pain and solitude were driving them all out of their minds, why weren't they screaming, but their screams froze in the icy air, her husband had told her that there were "so many things we will only understand when we're about to die" and she was ashamed because she still didn't understand anything, Judith Lange was no longer there to listen to her moan in silence, other suicides were expecting her in the night and while the lilac branch whipped the window Judith told her students about the throngs of Austrian schoolchildren who, forty years after, still filed through Mauthausen every day, all the horrors of Nazism were still in evidence there, they had to learn all about it, become fully conscious of it all, they had to see the executioner's instruments, drink the victims' blood, and Judith Lange's eyes were full of tears when she said you too must remember, you must not forget, and all they saw was the canopy of white lilacs out in the college yard and Judith Lange, sitting there so beautiful and serene, and they couldn't see the sense of resurrecting such a dim, morbid scene on such a beautiful day, a hundred and ten thousand people had died there, said Judith Lange, you'll never be able to forget it, not tonight, not tomorrow, never; some executioners were jovial, others were gentle, who knows, perhaps in eternity the tormentors were placed alongside their victims, perhaps a voice full of self-pity went on comforting those who were being led to the gas chamber: "If you only knew how it makes me suffer to see you suffer this way!" There had been nice, friendly tormentors who were good husbands and fathers, generous lovers, and yet they had left their descendants a Monument to Cruelty at Mauthausen; they had beaten, killed, massacred their fellow men with great pleasure, they were, Judith Lange said, God's skulking criminals, sometimes the executioners were so gifted they could assume the supplicating credulity of their victims; they too lifted their frightened faces to the sky as if to ask, "Can this possibly be happening to me?" — they had felt fear in the face of the incomprehensible cruelty that drove them to drunken orgies of blood, and even the tottering victims they nudged on towards the stairway of death had the nerve to sharpen that fear with a touching, pitiful cry, the victims dared to rise from the scalding nest of torture to face them, and when the sensitive executioner, who was a man just like any other, but an aesthete of pain, fearfully approached the neck that offered no resistance to his hands, something hovered in the bloody, moan-filled fog, something that was the very secret of agony, of death, and the sensitive executioner understood that he in turn, maybe tonight or tomorrow, would become that same feeble victim he had stunned with his blows and his hatred, and he was afraid, suddenly the perfection of his crime didn't seem to matter, he took his victim in his arms, sighed and stroked his head, "Don't be afraid, I don't want to hurt you," and the bewildered victim gazed up, a final glimmer of gratitude in his eye, it was almost love...but there were other executioners who were so sensitive that one never saw them — lacking the courage to kill with their own hands, they dispatched their invisible armies, their invisible massacre machines, and Judith Lange told them about it all, they stared at her without understanding, like the schoolchildren who visited Mauthausen day after day; Judith Lange also told them that everything had changed, that when trains passed near Mauthausen or any of the other torture sites a bloody steam rose from the ground, no, nothing was as before, the traveller comfortably seated or dozing in the train suddenly noticed the bloody vapour rising from the earth, and the victims' anguish was still so great that it shook the cars on the tracks and the passengers, suddenly oppressed, were covered with sweat and anguish, the anguish of a hundred and ten thousand victims clammy against their bones, they asked themselves why and where did it come from after so many years, but nothing was as before, the houses, the fields, the form of the trees, spring and summer alike it was winter in Mauthausen and wherever else a river of blood had run over the ground, forty years later you could still hear their cries and in the freight cars their emaciated bodies were still shrivelling up, but why, so long after, was it still going on, the countryside seemed as beautiful as ever, especially in spring and summer, you would have expected Austrian schoolchildren to be picking flowers and running in the fields as before in spite of what had happened there, but the schoolchildren, even if they didn't understand why, also felt fear rising in them when they drew near the site, they came in buses with their teachers, their brothers, their friends, they came to Mauthausen in order not to forget, they looked, they touched the instruments that had lacerated and crushed frail adolescent bodies, that had cut up the gleaming flesh that had been hands, arms, or cheeks, and the bloody vapour rose up and slowly seeped into the intact, triumphantly living flesh of the Austrian schoolchild who was only passing through Mauthausen, and the horror of all the evil inflicted on the victims was in him, and Judith Lange spoke of those who had been separated from each other, death was the greatest of pains but death had been preceded by the throes of separation, very often death closed in like something blind and deaf, sometimes it even came at the hands of a blind, deaf executioner, but those who watched their mothers, sisters, children, loved ones, or some part of themselves being taken away, went on living and breathing, still afflicted by the light of consciousness, the sharp awareness of what they were going to leave behind and lose forever, and that light, that consciousness, was something inexorable, who knows, said Judith Lange, maybe consciousness even preceded us in death, maybe it arrived before us to initiate us into the white light of nothingness that awaited us there, Judith Lange admitted that she too was afraid sometimes, for her consciousness always led her on, even drove her to consider sterile promises of eternity although she expected nothing from them except maybe that the executioners and their victims, united by divine justice, would find themselves face to face in the barren light of consciousness, but was that knowledge something to rejoice in? No — so if there were any happy expectations, they were to be found in life, in life as it was given us, we were life's path and refuge, our passing days were no more than that,

Judith Lange referred to moments of separation, the moment when the soul left the body, when people were separated from each other, the moment when the knife of ultimate torture severed all ties and the stray soul took off by itself, still under the shock of a terrible, savage evil, mothers wailed as their children were wrenched from their arms, the body perished when it was left deprived and thirsting for the one it was meant to love, and even those victims who were already marked for the gas chamber, already consumed by hunger and illness, began to tremble, for these final ties with the world, yes, the real world, these ties were also going to be taken from them and they would have absolutely nothing left on this earth that had already become unrecognizable, and as the day declined and the immensity of the grey sky turned harsh and furious, Florence rose laboriously, rose with the weight of the green suitcase still pulling her towards the ground, each step dragging her farther down and, far from everything, from everyone, she told herself she could perhaps go on walking a little more in the city, wandering, wandering, and she thought, "But it could happen to me too, being cold all winter, having to look at my frozen legs every night,..." she still had time to change, between that moment and the time of her death, time to transform herself Judith Lange had said, but how and why, and suddenly she noticed the shabby hotel, the Hôtel des Voyageurs, one of those places where you had to carry your own suitcase up to the seventh floor, no elevator, she was now buoyantly giddy at having fallen so low, she had never really had an existence of her own, living in the shadow of her powerful husband, but now she was aware of a kind of intensity, playing out the role she had assigned herself, advancing alone to realize the end of a life, even if it was just a life like hers that seemed so middle class and lucid, and Gloria told her she had a sick child who screamed sometimes but it was nothing serious, he'd get over it, "Go right on up, ma'am, make yourself at home, just follow that rag of a rug, it's just about worn through.... Oh, things were different in Luigi's time, we always had a good twenty thousand bucks in the bank... medicine gobbles it up like crazy, people got their troubles you know," muttered Gloria; perhaps she could see the port and the river from upstairs, something more than the plain grey sky, grey even if all of them kept saying what a nice day it was, and what were they all talking about, Florence asked herself as she entered the room, and oh, the shivering light of the electric bulb on the narrow, probably filthy bed, this she wasn't used to, she might be middle class but she was clean and lucid, but in the wan light of the bulb she saw that the bed wasn't so narrow after all, it was a mattress steeped in lechery, well, it was she who'd chosen it, it was all happening to her and not to someone else, she could have asked Gloria, "But what's the matter with your son, why this need to scream?" but she hadn't dared, she hadn't dared for so long now, there was a cold-water sink near the window, the hotel room told no lies, like Gloria it openly displayed its dissolute sighs, all the folds and creases of its sensual and moral misery, and that was just fine, thought Florence, if only she could learn courage here; later on, if her fear subsided a bit more, she would venture as far as the stairway, she would go and see how many squalid rooms like this there were in the hotel, a hundred maybe, she would find out who lived there, who had lived there, just who these people were that she had never even imagined, artists, strays, or destitutes like herself, how ignominious it was to live in such conditions and yet men had always lived this way, there was no emergency exit, it was a fire-trap and, all alone, she began to tremble, asking herself why she should be trembling so for no apparent reason, but her arrival in this place had suddenly cut her off from everything that only yesterday she had still loved, there was nothing left to weigh her down, she was free, and yet a distant force made her body shake violently, overpowered her like a mocking, taunting hand whose power, however, was no less abstracted than the hand of God. There was a feeling, thought Florence, which obsessed us all, the feeling of things repeating themselves, the oppressive weight of the mysteries in our lives, the question of how to scale the walls of this pit in which everything, even the simplest gesture, had been decided for us, get up, sit down, all of it determined beforehand; it hadn't been so very long ago that she had accompanied her husband to some perfectly elegant, inane hotel — they had been in Europe for an international congress of physicists and she had had no idea what they were all talking about — and she had abruptly sought refuge in a murky den, a bar on the ground floor of the hotel, and there her minute existence breathed for itself alone; she had a book in her hand, familiar company, something written by a stranger that somehow sublimated the triviality of her own life and then they'd barged in on her tranquillity, a group of young people of no specific age — they must have been between

fifteen and eighteen and their parents had come with them
to their first ball — attired in tuxedos, or silk dresses with
plunging necklines, emblems of the traditional values of
their parents, or rather of the crumbling of those values
that no longer had any spiritual roots; superficial, splendid,
degenerate, they paced the sumptuous salons with disdainful, childish faces, their eyes already dulled; if their
parents' ideals had taken the form of possessions — of
Mercedes, of precious stones or swimming pools — the
dreams, at least, had often been engendered by hardship
and misery, while these youths, thought Florence, didn't
even dream, they were merely the puppets of their parents' desires, pale ghosts of their elders, emptiness order-
ing the same martinis and wearing the same hairdos as
their parents, but all of a sudden one student had distinguished himself from the uniformly gloomy group, staring
Florence straight in the eye as though he were calling for
help, and she had sat there, her book on her lap, fighting to
contain the convulsive trembling of her soul, he was a
skinny boy with long hands and he looked at her as if to
ask, "Can one possibly live like this? Is this my future?"
The boy seemed on the verge of suffocation, cooped up in
binding clothes, and yet he'd said nothing, had just given
Florence this anxious look to which she hadn't been able
to respond since she too had been afraid, and Judith Lange
explained to her students that faith in the world — a
passion far removed from indifference which, on the
contrary, is nothing but passion kindled by terror — would
flower in those who still longed for an ideal; but they were
impatient and frivolous, they gazed at the branch of white
lilac in the college yard, why bring up terror on such a

lovely day, in Stuttgart a minister and his wife had just buried their daughter, victim of that terror to which the young girl had perhaps devoted all her innocence and her faith just as her parents had devoted theirs, loyally, feverishly, to God's commandments, you must not kill, they had instructed her from early childhood, you must not steal what belongs to others, you must respect life, must not kill, must not kill; she'd obeyed for a long time but one day — who knows, maybe she'd been afflicted by the world's ugliness, maybe the minister's daughter had also experienced this fearful trembling that puts an end to all certainty — the pure serene forehead of the child had clouded over with guilty musings, redeeming blood with blood, shedding blood to revenge blood already shed, and now good, loving parents were burying a daughter who had suddenly turned bad and left the world burdened not only with the terrible fatalities of suicide and crime but also with the accusation of men who disowned her. Perhaps the minister's daughter had suddenly become capable of doing horrendous things as she passed by Mauthausen or Terezin, places that had become, even though they weren't world-famous for the crimes that had been committed there, valleys of tears for those who had perished there by the hundreds, by the thousands, and maybe the minister's daughter had passed close by and had heard their muffled wails while a bloody, slimy vapour shrouded the apparently lifeless countryside which crouched there silently, its trees bare; a long time, a very long time before we were born, and while we were growing up, despotic generations had outraged human dignity and humanity could not forget it, the victims' corpses were restless in the grave of time, said Judith Lange, and other generations, born of terror, gave birth to terror and to a liturgy of violence and death that would be implacable, for these children were the fruits of shame, the shame and the infamy of their parents; Judith Lange asked her students if they realized that they might represent the last wave of humanity to pass over the earth, no, why, they asked, and there were white lilacs in the sun, in the yard, no, why, many others like the minister's daughter would choose exile, death or that snuffing out of the self which is so easy to accomplish, because that choice is born of the breath of agony, the inspiration that suddenly strikes those who are already conscious of the dangers surrounding them; and Judith fell silent, for her distracted students weren't listening any more, she had hung Kierkegaard's portrait on the wall of her room and now it came to her mind; she would come home at night and the gentle, ascetic face would remind her that the age of blood had been preceded by a peaceful, enticing era in which thoughts were directed, unhindered and fecund, to noble, arid heights, she thought of Pascal, his features bearing witness to the ravages of God in a soul that had been consumed by coldness before its time; in spite of every-thing there had been epochs in which men could think and create, bound by rigorous lines of thought and the feroci-ous glare projected by disdainful minds, but that time was past and now our heavy, guilty gestures tagged along after us, Florence was pacing the hotel room and asking herself, "Can there be one free person in the whole world?" Didn't we all have to become invincible, hateful, just to survive? Hatred. She understood it in a flash: hatred was what

happened when you were fed up with love and commiser-
ation, hatred was a necessary, voluntary act, and suddenly
she had the impression that it wasn't helplessness that was
making her tremble, but rather the morbid, indispensable
hatred she'd just acquired, and she wondered what monstrous quirk of fate, what conspiracy against herself had
destined her to life on a planet which was all threats and
terror, on this spineless, skinless earth where she had
unfortunately taken root, they always insisted that it was
better to live than to have never existed but the soul
craving for justice had no proof of that, and then Florence
heard a sudden commotion outside and ran to the window, there was something going on down the street, it
didn't concern her and yet it was happening right there,
close by, a child had been hit by an ambulance, it had only
grazed him and now he was sitting on the sidewalk
surrounded by policemen, apparently more astonished
than hurt, all the same, you still protected some beings
instinctively, elderly people and children, the dazed child
let himself be picked up by unfamiliar hands and the
ambulance swallowed him up, you could no longer see
him, you only knew that he hadn't been injured, just
frightened or shaken by the fear others had felt for him,
even Florence in the distance had felt her hands and
forehead clammy with sweat, fear was suddenly watching
disaster strike you when you couldn't understand it,
Florence shut the window, she was safe, sheltered, in the
next room a couple quarrelled, they lashed out at each
other with raging pain, hatred, hatred, their hatred wring-
ing sobs and shouts from them, it was the form their
stupefied, bruising love had taken, perhaps this same

insidious love would claim them as its smiling victims later on, in an hour or later that night, but it was still daylight and they were hungry, they had lived in misery for a long time and they craved the torture, the commanding hatred that helped them forget all other misfortunes, their presence reassured her, their hatred-turned-love set fire to the existence of Florence who was frightened and alone — no helpful, violent hand would come to embrace or strike her, nobody was doing her any good or harm now, what feelings could an indifferent, bitter adult stir up, what could you provoke by falling from the seventh floor of a sordid hotel? Nothing, not even the solicitude of the policemen who'd carried the child to the ambulance, the child was unscathed but they defended and protected him, society still had these ramparts of pity, our hatred lay dormant while we rushed to defend and protect those weaker than ourselves, Florence, a woman who had had her own particular beauty, her particular defects, would be down there, her broken body still arched in pain, and they wouldn't come running to pity and protect, who knows, maybe they would come in anger and envy, cursing her for it, she had nothing but contempt for all of them, and this hatred comforted her, it was the voluptuousness of the dying, our crushed, beaten bodies assuaged by this harvest of violence and hatred, it had to be that way, we were such weak creatures, being born and dying in anger, suicide was not only a choice but a punishment as well, an exaltation, suicide was the ultimate exaltation of your own nothingness, but how do you bring life to a close and cross the dark passage, oh my God, my God, but the lovers in the next room suddenly calmed down, now they were speaking in hushed tones, maybe they were kissing, where did they come from, who were they, they emerged, rising up from the hollow cavern of hatred, of love, they loved each other in muffled tones, reconciled and close maybe; a boy on a bike had smiled contentedly at Florence in passing, contented, yes, like all those small consolations that pass through our lives and disappear, she too had been offered contented tenderness and yet this passage was so dark, so dark for all of them, it was spring for Judith Lange but for Florence winter would drag on and on, melancholic, heavy, and endless, she stretched out on the bed, thinking she might sleep, that devouring hatred had exhausted her, it was a form of passion that suddenly ate into you but it was healthy, maybe all these extremes we harbour are healthy, all that is so sick with pain, with threatening intensity, even what we call our happiness, she thought, for tomorrow we'll no longer be here to experience it and the ghost of happiness lost will wander on alone, without us, uninhabited, wandering, wandering; then Florence realized she was falling asleep, her heart was beating slowly, worn out by hatred, she dreamed of all that she loved, that always seemed so intangible when maybe that was what reality was, something directed her steps and her memory very precisely towards an oriental garden she had admired for its organization and design, it might have been part of a Chinese painting for Florence had spent her life in museums and she felt good in them, she waited patiently in these places where her wait was fortified and nourished by the unerring values of other epochs, by things that had happened to others but that her eyes could still perceive, her eyes were the eyes of an invisible person and they went unnoticed in museums where time preserved its images, its men and the trappings of their lives; paintings taught her that a buried world would remain visible to her for a long time yet, painting was an art for captives like Florence, things that no longer existed became visible and transparent on canvas; in her dreams the oriental garden was still in its place, she herself was somewhere else, sitting in front of a mountain chalet in some North American countryside, the oriental garden comforted her from afar and she was reassured by the indulgence of its oriental characters, by their delicate, distant offering, while close by a jovial lumberjack was chopping, chopping wood, Florence gazed softly into the distance towards the strawberry fields, they too were neat and tidy, she had the impression she'd drawn them herself, the strawberries before her eyes were as clear and tempting as the vivid fruit seen in paintings, no longer painted but reanimated, spontaneously coming to life in the almost tasty light the artist had conceived for them alone, and Florence felt a great peace, she had come into contact with the simplicity of her inner existence, perhaps it would have been a peaceful one if it hadn't been for human knowledge and contacts, for thus projected, all by yourself in an incorruptible space, wasn't each of us the master of that uninhabited region, couldn't you fill it, in spite of everything, with the pureness of your simplest desires? The oriental characters, mythical and yet so real for Florence, filed past between hedges of flowers, bowing from afar, offering to share their delicate dishes with her, but Florence turned her head as if to show them that she was no longer hungry, it was too late now for hunger and thirst and yet it would have pleased her to join them; she trusted them completely, but she perceived the milky whiteness in the background as a symptom of death and the white in her dreams, thought Florence, was the lie in the blood, it was the sign that death was present in one form or another, red was something blameable but it meant passion and violence, which she recognized, while white, milk, snow, everything white, was a lie, was blood that hadn't yet spilled over, it disguised itself as innocence and accused her and then suddenly she was awake, still moved by the peace that had carried her so far away, she noticed for the first time that the door to her room was ajar, why hadn't she noticed it earlier when she'd realized, as soon as she had come into the room, that there was no emergency exit, and then someone came in, a young man about her son's age, twenty-five maybe, but he wasn't an honest, short-haired young man like her son who was preparing his Ph.D. in an American university, no, this one was an obtuse, sensual thing without a name, a creature chance had sent to her; come on in, she said, don't be afraid, maybe she could pass her fear along to someone else, shut herself up in this danger with him, he approached her, her body, began to talk to her, explaining that he didn't want to be alone, you'll see, I won't hurt you, he said, and she replied that she believed him, he didn't know how to express what he felt, maybe he felt nothing more than what he was expressing now — a bit of hunger, a bit of thirst — he too had the impression he was wandering alone, poor boy, he inwardly called himself, but why not if it meant one last thrill of life, and he lingered on near her, with her, telling her she was still beautiful, still alive, she was no longer afraid, she thought, she had the courage of those who are about to die, such dizziness, with her husband she'd often felt annihilated by the breath of helplessness or the servile nature of her passion but she felt none of that now, this was something entirely different, a dizziness, and she was bored, completely overpowered by an oppressing boredom, she was bored with the man, the passage of time was suspended, it was love, just landing on her without movement or flight, a man who was teaching her boredom in all its fatality, its horror, the insipidity of dead moments that had just invaded her being, how could she have known that boredom was such a humiliating trial, always before she'd been taken, charmed, bewitched, she'd been able to die and be reborn in another's arms and now boredom suddenly became something libidinous, pervasive, a monster and she was shut in with it, and yet the young man was charming, he wasn't hurting her at all, he was just there, covering her with his boredom, he had no idea how petrifying the mission he'd been charged with was, and as she watched him dress near the window, in a light that made him appear naked and vulnerable all of a sudden, Florence began to pity his existence, his particular reality in which she could in no way participate, this being who would go on living, alone, without her; his jeans clung to his body like a second skin, blue and corroded, he was a charming young man even if he was a bit of a lout, she just wasn't used to acting this way, letting a man who'd go without even telling her his first name cuddle up against her misery, all the same she felt, as he was about to leave, that she'd already been delivered of him, of the sickness and boredom he had implanted in her, and she felt sorry for that part of him she still retained in herself, and in the intimacy of this room she pitied the smell of his greasy hair, his cheeks sunken in the light, and the envelope of cocaine he wanted to share with her — he sniffed a bit of it, anxiously, parsimoniously, and she observed a slight flush in his cheeks as he shut himself up alone in the zone of his dreams where she could never again reach him, he blurted out a few obscure words, smiled at her without seeing her and then left the room, his step already lost, what's the use of closing the door, thought Florence, who knows, something might happen to her yet, perhaps life stirred even in the depths of terror and this room answered all the cries that passed it, echoed them like an abyss, Florence went down the stairs alone — the body's engine kept up its feverish activity right to the end, commanding, exacting from you the same unconscious discipline as always — and sitting down on the stairs she waited, who were they, yes, who were these people, those who lived here, here or elsewhere on this earth on which she was about to put an end to her exile? — she leaned against the ramp and listened, observed, quiet, all of a sudden she felt perfectly calm in her nest of terror, and down below old Tim was telling Gloria that his hosts — old age and death — were waiting for him at the poorhouse, he'd be just fine there, yes, fed, housed, he'd given up on Ireland, *"The bastards, the bastards,"* he muttered, crying, but he wasn't thinking about Ireland, he was thinking about his dog Tim, his brother, his family, his hearth and home, Tim whom he had dragged to the pound on a rope, and Gloria shook him, saying, "Please, don't cry, a dog's life is like a man's life, comes to an end one day or another, drink your beer and shut up!" But Gloria had also loved Tim the dog more than Tim the man, Tim the dog was a noble, honourable animal while Tim the Irishman was a "pig and a damned drunkard", Gloria said, and why did one have to go before the other, especially since Tim the dog's existence had been blameless while old Tim had led a "smutty, trashy life, yeah, you should be ashamed, old man!" And Florence listened to Tim talk about his dog, groan over his own abandonment and that of the creature he'd led towards its incomprehensible end, and she thought I'm afraid, I'm afraid, for she became now Tim the Irishman, now Tim the dog, they both had or would have, today or tomorrow, a similar, tragic end, no, she reflected, the victims couldn't understand, they hadn't been granted this gift, this clair-voyance that would have helped them understand why they were being punished, we were destroyed so quickly, stoned to death, Tim the Irishman and his dog might just as well be called Florence for they were, like her, subjected to the violence of the supreme tormentors and these executioners were gifted with supernatural cruelty, all that the visible world could perceive was our execution, our death, the one who had passed on left behind a stagnant, often painful gap, an empty space that no longer contained his voice, his cries, but only a disquieting silence, and this silence was proof that a man had lived there in a space of his own, a space that had marked off the limits of his days, his nights; and Florence, like Tim and his dog, might also be called Job, they said God had had no pity on Job, desolate, Job had been submitted to every conceivable misfortune, to every bodily and spiritual torture and to a death which had perhaps degraded both his soul and his body, Tim the dog was all that, his brother the man was also all that, poor Tim, poor dog, thought Florence, both of them caught in the angry storm, but Tim the dog finally rested in peace and might not this buried animal's soul represent a sacrificial incense, might it not, who knows, redeem our cowardice, our crimes? You could find nothing to reproach our sleeping, unconscious beasts for, they had brought us nothing but happiness, and yet we behaved towards them exactly the way our invisible executioners — who alone had the power to decide when to massacre us — behaved towards us, we were the masters of our animals and they our slaves, in happiness and suffering alike, we determined their extermination and their disappearance; old Tim couldn't say whether or not all that was true, his words weren't clear or well defined, the only language he knew was blasphemy, that was the way he hated or loved, he cursed himself for having loved his dog so much and in the same way he cursed himself for having done away with him, he cursed Tim for not being there any more at his side, his muzzle white with drool, but Florence experienced these feelings in his stead for she was unhappy but lucid and the flame of consciousness was something so cold that everywhere, the world, nature, all living things, everything around her was hibernating with her and she was afraid, because it was no longer a sensation of fear but fear itself that had lodged itself in her, perhaps for all eternity, for when you left this world it was probably only to enter another equally full of lies; where was Tim the dog now, vanished, wandering in some other place with his fear, his ills, along with thousands of other phantoms just like himself, and now Tim — missing the dog he had so often hounded with insults but with whom he had nonetheless shared his last crust of bread, a battered sandwich they'd eaten together in the park, in the sun, *"Tim, my old bastard, where are you now, you monster?"* — Tim thought of Ireland in the summer, of all the lambs he had seen in the green fields as a child, he had never seen that kind of verdant beauty anywhere except in his country, that was paradise, all the lambs bouncing around in the light, but like Tim the dog they had become, one day not very long after their birth, victims on our altar; suddenly one morning they had passed from their gay leaping, from the frolic of their innocent emotion, to factories where they had had their throats cut at dawn and neither the verdant meadows nor the unfeeling, soft blue sky remembered their lamentations, still less the streams of blood splashing the factory walls, and Tim the Irishman knew all that, he couldn't ignore it any more having worked as an executioner in those very death factories; fortunately modern technology had spared Tim the dog such suffering but all the same, thought Florence, our competence in destroying others doesn't stave off the fear; when old Tim thought about his dog it wasn't his death-agony that haunted him — there had been none, just one shot of instant death and the victim was immediately struck down, trusting in his annihilation — what haunted old Tim was the look in the old dog's eyes, yes, thought Florence, that flame of consciousness, it was so cold and whether it came from a man or a beast you recognized the gnawing despair, the same instinct, the dread, nothing seemed more formidable to us than that gleam of consciousness, the most unendurable physical suffering simply faded away before the fear that seized us, the fear of no longer existing, dread of nothingness or of the vast, devastating unknown, and even Tim the dog had understood that as he tagged along behind Tim on the end of his rope, he had understood it all, it was the light of understanding that killed men and animals long before the onslaught of death itself, and old Tim remembered the knowing look the dog had given him, the sudden, inescapable consciousness in the eye, he would never forget it, it would persecute him day and night from now on, for old Tim too would soon go off to the poorhouse; and Florence also felt the dog's gaze upon her at that moment in which everything around takes on a chilling, luminous consciousness, and when the light of consciousness suddenly descends upon all things, it was then, she thought, that one understood how transparent pain was, or rather it was she, Florence, who became transparent, her hands, her eyes, her body no longer defended her against this transparency of the cold, her entire being was vibrant with this coldness, this solitude, with other people's misfortunes, Tim's, his dog's, their troubles passed right through her, there was no longer anything to protect her, her muscles, nerves, and bones were aching, her entire body imbued with the acute, steeled consciousness, and she knew she would never get over it even if she decided to go on living, we were so rarely conscious, she thought, of the distinct panic produced by the beating of our hearts and the agitation of our nerves but all of a sudden we were, consciousness set itself in motion somewhere inside us, forcing us to listen to our bodies' subterranean quiverings, and it was a motion that allowed no halt or repose, now she was no longer sure where reality began and where it left off, her nights set fire to her days, the awareness of being alive tore through her entire being, she was at once dazzled and destroyed by the violence of it, by the lancing of her memories, it broke in on her peace upheaving it like one of those cold winds that sweep the desert, just when she'd thought she was alone under the sheets, completely withdrawn into the secret of her abandonment, of her stark misery, suddenly strange people started coming in, dead or alive, they came wearing masks and colours, forcing their voices and their gestures upon her, there was Tim the dog, Tim the man, and the youth who had offered her his ration of cocaine, who knows what would become of them all, she opened the door to love and hell, she was afraid, that was her story, just that and nothing more, but they didn't know it, and while she was still sitting on the stairs, old Tim had suddenly stopped sobbing, he'd reminisced about old times, where were those times now, but old Tim was talking about wild horses that no whip had ever broken, they strayed, strayed freely in that nostalgic nature that we alone perhaps can so describe in words, even if they're only the drunken words of old Tim, the wild horses strayed but the brick orphanage in which Tim had spent the first years of his life remained solidly immovable, neither the orphanage nor the nuns nor the sea had moved at all; old Tim, who could possibly imagine that this bespittled mug had once been a little boy, Tim, running along those same rough beaches and leaping from rock to rock at dawn before mass, and a bit later, he remembered it was a bit later, still wandering in the late afternoon before the evening sky fell to the rages of night

— but the warmth of the water was so soothing then and the orphans plunged fully dressed, shouting, into the grey and blue splendour that enticed them, caressed them, drowned their most shameful distresses, swept them towards mad passion, rebellious force — and then, it must have been late, Tim, that other Tim whom no one in this world or any other remembered, had lain beside a woman on one of those rocks that had been burned black by the water, the cold and the sun of the country, that's what Ireland was, he said, he must have been ugly then, puny and shivering with cold in his salt-smelling rags; the vision he'd kept of himself, however, was just a discordant vibration in space, in his own space, the sacred space that had belonged to Tim the orphan when he went out from his brick orphanage in the morning, and yet he felt that his image was coming back to him, embellished and fervent, for he especially recalled the woman lying at his side: they didn't speak, they weren't touching, but the world's din had been silenced around them, they were there, destiny calling both of them to this place and the mute sensuality of the scenery that warmed them, reconciling all that was foreign and perhaps unreconcilable in them, and even that was a falsehood, like the rest; in spite of their salty odour the rags of old Tim who had once been that orphan on the beach gave off a biting, exciting perfume, the fervour, yes, of being there with a woman who knew nothing about him beyond what she perceived of attractive youth, knew nothing of the misfortunes that had already begun to deposit their layer of scabs and devastation on him, but saw just him, Tim, a body in the sun, his clothes washed and spread out around him, with golden drops and salt tracing paths on his white shoulders and torso. Tim was dreaming gently, perhaps he would forget the silent agony of Tim the dog for an hour or so, and Florence asked herself if the death-agony of human beings didn't begin when they lost all desire, when like herself they no longer expected anything, confronted only with a vast wasteland on which they could walk and run, but it was a vastness without horizon, the sensation of moving ahead or turning back towards its frosty mountains was a neutral, indifferent sensation, there was no longer any way to hide or escape, no cracks or crevices in the hard, icy ground, the only thing you could sink into was your own débâcle, but Florence, who had been living for a long time under the illusion of waiting for something, discovered she was no longer waiting for anything, and no familiar look could touch her there where she'd taken refuge; and yet in the dark, ignorant depths of old Tim's memory there was the sea, a rock, a woman, a kind of consolation that drifted in from far back to nudge away the difficulty he found in living in the present, and Florence wondered if there was some way to discover that intensity once again, that fever of expectation, she would dress for the evening, yes, that was it, she would light a cigarette and wait for her husband in some elegant hotel, a book on her knees, and he wouldn't arrive, or maybe he'd be late, he'd come in, just as considerate as always to her, with the gestures she knew so well, he'd take her by the hand for suddenly that was what the waiting game was; you made believe that you didn't know anything about yourself, about the nightly resentments or the petty revenges that hang heavy on everyday life, suddenly none of that existed, you metamorphosed yourself, became the person someone was waiting for, and the other player knew all about this game of seduction — as human beings weren't we above all malleable, greedy beasts, worshipping each other's alluring gestures, the invitations to pleasure? — we achieved this sensual magic by casting a spell on ourselves, it was pleasant to wait for some agreeable person in some agreeable place, he would be attractively dressed and it was called living in style or having a taste for life, it came naturally, thought Florence, it was delightful and we spoke of it as our everyday wait, the only thing that slipped our minds was that this artful, delicious arrangement of our habits, our agreeable habits at any rate, was not eternal, that one night or another the husband, the son, lover, or whatever apparition put an end to our wait, would no longer be there and there would be emptiness in his place; when you were Florence and when you dressed in the evening it was in vain, you found yourself face to face with the tranquil nothingness that lurked everywhere, at the bottom of a stairway or behind a door, maybe the cruellest part of it, she thought, was realizing just that, knowing that however strong her desire, however acute her memory, he would never come back, would never again come down those stairs, knowing also that we had no power over that absence, but there was yet a worse side to it, which was knowing that the living substance of the one we no longer expected, the substance we had sensually embraced and loved, that fraternal substance that had been joined to ours, had disappeared but was still alive elsewhere, knowing that and feeling the vast wasteland of silence settling in over the scorching flames we had kindled so closely that we ourselves had been consumed by them. Florence was one of those old-fashioned, out-dated people with no self-complacency, one of those people, she thought, who love only one person at a time, on principle rather than by virtue, one person in one lifetime; she had loved her husband more than anyone else, according to her way of thinking at any rate, her entire ability to love had been lavished on him; wasn't that a great deal in itself, she asked herself, when you consid-ered the stinginess of the human heart, and now, she pondered, that same love to which she had brought a total, religious voracity was nothing more than smoke in the desert, an illusive hint of happiness, while its object, the most solitary of animals, had at least thought to find refuge elsewhere, avoiding our curses, our odour, or the breath of our sickness — and that was the moment when everyone abandoned us; that was how Florence who had, according to her own former criteria, been a lovely and distinguished woman living in her own world with the costly illusion of being a proud part of it, that was how the same Florence came to be sitting on a miserable staircase where nobody — nobody of her race, she thought, for she envisioned an entire race disappearing with her — where nobody except maybe a rat or a sick child would come to lay his mute chagrin at her side, and suddenly she had a glimpse of her utter solitude, saw herself even more alone than on the stairs where her feeble existence was waning like a glimmer, but it was an invisible gleam and that was comforting, she saw herself again, so alone and lost in restaurants that were built like huge ships, she was all alone there in the middle of a river, a river adrift; at such times the lightest step burst into infinite space and sound, a lone flower in a vase was enough to jar our exasperated, vanquished senses like a stroke of crazed lightning, and all that, all that which frightened her when she thought about it, oh yes, that was a fever far more dangerous than the shivers of anguish she felt, sitting on the stairs, for here, who knows, maybe the rat or Gloria's sick child would come, maybe they would come wordlessly to accompany her right up to the threshold of the forbidden, and it was so strange when she thought of the man she had loved, her acute, spiteful lucidity didn't recognize the man but rather his hand, his arm, or some part of his body that had touched her forever — those who rose from the dead went on living in us that way, their resurrection was slow and measured, an arm, a hand, a sex whose slowness had outplayed all caprice, and this resurrected man or woman pushed us along our dark, fecund, and audacious path. Florence, feeling the rustle of these incessant resurrections all around her, wondered if it wouldn't be healthier just to no longer exist, to annihilate hope and resurrection along with herself, do away with that living, palpable matter that was still so attractive that it had unknowingly begun to devour you, and then she remembered Judith Lange, that too was strange, Florence was drawn to empty lecture halls, she filled the empty spaces by herself, with her unfulfilled distinction, with her intelligence — so bound up in reflection, in a penetrating spirit — which nobody understood, for in these vacant places, in the empty lecture halls, you saw no more than her glance, you spoke to her about Egyptian art and she understood everything, the truth, her eyes and her hands spoke, she knew how to listen, how to understand, she had pondered it all and emptiness no longer frightened her, and unexpectedly Judith Lange had been there, like a summer sun in her desert, and she also listened, Florence smiled scornfully at her, she felt utterly indifferent, she was going to die soon, yet Judith was there, she didn't understand anything about Egyptian art but she was lovely and serene, and how could you help giving her a smile, however indifferent or scornful; Florence was afraid but at the same time she was convinced of her superiority over others since she could thus abandon herself to the deep dangers of consciousness: it seemed to her that nobody else was capable of taking such an exact measure of personal loss and terror, and who was that little Judith Langenais after all, something of the child still showing in her eyes, what could she possibly perceive of our ills, but Florence had smiled at her out of curiosity, scornful but still curious about others because, she thought, curiosity isn't what ties us to life and then, provocative, she'd spoken to her about Egyptian art, she knew all there was to know about it for it was like the opaque visage of the death she carried in herself; she asked Judith, who was listening, gentle and attentive, if she hadn't noticed the heads with empty eyes in these museums, eyeless because the face was elsewhere, the face was a tomb, but Judith Lange was perfectly ignorant about such things and Florence, still curious, sad with the scorn and indifference that overwhelmed her, suddenly said tell me about yourself, what is it like to live with a peaceful soul? and Judith Lange refused to talk about herself, she spoke of history's murders, but why you, Florence asked, you weren't even born in '39, in '45, we're here now though, said Judith Lange, but Florence was no longer listening, the deluge of grave reflections, heavy as stones, aggravated her affliction and she looked at the radiant, healthy girl, her clear, bright look, the white, eager teeth, my God, why was she talking about these things that didn't concern her, what criminal ancestors had already clouded her innocence, her brightness, and Florence said no, stop speaking, stop it girl, you have no right to say these things, I do, yes, in my case it's different, she would take Judith's mind off it, I can speak of them, about everything, I'm beyond it all, nothing lies ahead of me but sometimes I like to think that these empty places are waiting for me and I hang around vacant train stations, it's for the other trip, the one nobody mentions, Judith Lange told Florence their paths would cross again, in a train station maybe, and then she had to go, her students were expecting her to go to a demonstration, which, and why, asked Florence but Judith was no longer there, this brief contact with the girl had given her such warmth that Florence was afraid she would recover the will to live, and that couldn't, mustn't, come back, ever, nothing fated to die can survive the light of consciousness; and yet Judith seemed to enjoy living, perhaps it was the strength of youth, but how criminal those ancestors seemed who had already blackened the hearts and minds of people who might otherwise have been refreshed by new acquaintances, her son, for example, who would probably become a physicist like his father, had never mentioned history's murders to her, maybe he'd been born to commit others; thinking of the power of science gave Florence the shivers, when science didn't take man's comfort as its aim it became a form of art, but the art of terror, she thought, she'd been in awe of her husband's brain, sometimes, imagining what was preparing itself right there beneath the unruffled forehead, behind the grey eyes, she had trembled with fear, as if all human thoughts, an army of men, and all the mechanisms of the Great Terror were gathered there, already forming a terrible future. Then Florence recalled a forgotten moment, a moment lost somewhere in herself — she had probably stumbled in her bewilderment and perhaps Judith had noticed from a distance the grey spot of her body against the grey background of the deserted station, she'd taken her home, she'd asked her what she usually did at night, you see, Judith, I do what I'm doing now, I open a book on my knees, very often I don't read because there are no real words in it and I'm afraid, said Florence, then sometimes there's television in the evening, I stare into that space that talks about us, about our tragedies and misfortunes, from a great, a very great distance, there's no picture, it's absent but I'm afraid, if you only knew, I'm frightened, but you're too young, you can't understand, Judith Lange listened intently and Florence smiled, she was afraid she'd start crying, laughing, those terrible mockeries, the bitterness on the tip of her tongue, but she mustn't, her words were being carefully followed, I'm Doctor Gray's wife, Florence said, but Judith hadn't heard, she was glancing through the book whose words were absent, Florence by her side, she was explaining what was going on in front of her eyes: what one calls television, Judith was saying, serious all of a sudden, is our own way of seeing, our reflection, we are there, Judith said, we see ourselves, we assist at birth and agony — "Why do you see all these things I don't?" asked Florence jealously, why you, it's not fair, she was about to insult Judith even though she hardly knew her, she had to hurt someone, Judith Lange was looking at that thing that reflects us, that monstrous object of contemporary life, thought Florence in a rage, exasperated, for the young woman was forcing on her the obligation to live and think that she had refused for so long, and who was she after all, she knew nothing about Egyptian art, maybe she knew something about philosophy, an anarchist with changing ideas, and yet there was something so gentle about her, how could you put her out of your home, you know, Florence said, I don't like other people, for me they're like another book with the words missing, I don't expect them any more, they no longer expect me, we all live in absence, I've just finished paying my debts to the world and you've just begun to make yours, I'd be afraid if I were you, what's going on on television, what are all these empty images and dialogues about, and Judith Lange explained that a man was about to be hanged, but why are you crying, asked Florence, it's only a movie, they're going to hang him because he refuses to kill, to go to war, look, the executioner is coming now, his eyes won't see anything more beneath the blindfold, why are you crying, all that happened before you were born, said Florence, my strength, she added vigorously, my strong point is that I never cry; then suddenly she retreated to a corner of the room and broke out sobbing, hard, Judith didn't budge, she understood Florence's cry, her moan, perhaps she had even imagined the outburst, maybe it was just a silent retreat, a mute wail, at any rate Judith hadn't fled and

Florence looked at her, thinking that maybe she was just as absent as the others, although her presence somehow toned down the fear, and yet she didn't dare approach Judith, it would mean living again, and she remained coiled up in her own thoughts, keeping strictly to herself and thinking my God, my God, don't have mercy on me, please don't offer me the faintest glimmer of that kind of pity, it's too late, and it was too late, Judith was no longer there, who knows, maybe she'd also been transpierced by the same gleam of consciousness, Florence or Judith, who was to say which was the child of the Apocalypse, both of them perhaps when you got down to it, death was not the only thing that kept us apart, while life united us against our will, and Florence had the crazy idea that if she saw Judith again, Judith with her healthy, vital glow, she might want to live but it was an insane desire, just one of those absurd dreams that haunt us, perhaps Judith was right after all when she saw the smoke of the crematorium rising everywhere, it was true that adults had forgotten, for they were indifferent and orderly, as was Florence even in her conception of death, there was a strict, severe order to it all, maybe Judith was also right in believing that the greatest criminals were those who enjoyed order, wisdom, sometimes even goodness, that their crimes had been carefully contained in chemical cells in which all was order and pure reality, the pure reality of duty, wasn't the duty of crime a duty like any other, maybe Judith was right, thought Florence, sitting on the steps of her miserable hotel, yes, maybe she was right when she heard voices everywhere that sang of mourning and destruction while the sacrificial smoke infested a dead, indifferent world, that was it, history weighed heavily on Judith Lange's shoulders, she'd been born so late, too late, but she was there and she resisted, determined to perfect some furious, intelligent form of resistance, were they all deaf, she couldn't be the only one who heard it all, could she, and she had told Florence that musicians were sometimes spared in the camps, celestial voices might survive the terror for a day, a night, and the voices, the lamentations of our terror-stricken victims, had been inspired by extremely orderly men, Florence had heard her out to the end, she was no longer smiling, she was alone on the stairs and he was approaching her, it wasn't the famished rat she'd been expecting while staring at the vomit stains on the rug, "that rag of a rug" Gloria had spoken of which had its own long story, it was one of so many objects we subjected to our needs and wants, to our cowardly acts, and now he was walking over vomit stains on the rug like Jesus on the muddy waters, Jesus whose story she'd never liked for he didn't exist, while the human being who was coming towards her did, Gloria's son surely, with a bandage sitting like a white crown on his head, it was a white crown and Florence, who didn't like white in her dreams, was frightened, he spoke with clumsy, aborted, barely pronounced words, explained that his mother had sent him with this food, it was a plate of burned spaghetti, you must eat, she'd said, and Florence asked why, Mike seemed to say because my mother said so although he just looked at Florence without speaking, handing her the plate that repulsed her, and then he repeated eat, my mother said to, his cheeks were sunken, his eyes burning but he didn't appear to be suffering, perhaps he wasn't the sick child Gloria had mentioned after all; aloof, he told Florence almost indifferently about Tim the dog's death, of course it was sad but hundreds of them died that way every day, then he told her once again to eat and as she watched him turn to go downstairs he tapped his head and laughed, saying, "Mom's crazy to bandage me up this way, you'd think I was a baby and that's not true, they pulled a tooth because of the treatment at the hospital, it's better not to have too many teeth, they stick tubes in your mouth. . . ." No, no I can't eat, said Florence, pushing away the plate Mike had offered, eat it anyway, he said in the same dry tone, it was because of his teeth that he had trouble speaking, she thought, because of the fresh, bloody holes at the bottom of his mouth, what's your name, but he hadn't known how to answer, had just said eat it while it's still good, "Mom made it for you, she always looks after her guests," what's your name, Florence repeated and once again the image of the nimble bike-rider who had glanced at her came back, it wasn't Mike though but an athletic boy who was going to live, and live a long time perhaps; she knew nothing about this one who had brought her a plate of foul-smelling, burned spaghetti with an awful taste, and yet she ate to please him, lowering her eyes with disgust, Michel, Michel Agneli, "Mike, the others call me, Jojo's downstairs, I've still got to rock her and Lucia will be coming in, all the dishes are waiting to be washed. . . ." And your father, asked Florence, no father, "and what for, anyway, we've got five police dogs. . . ." Misfortune's implacable fatality, Florence thought as she listened to Mike, here too there was some mysterious coherence, some kind of order, as she swallowed the food she realized she was hungry, maybe even famished but fear was stronger than the most exacting appetites, perhaps he won't come back, she thought, no, I couldn't stand seeing him again with the white cloth around his head, for she'd felt such fear for him, he was just a tender victim and tender victims were so quickly crushed, they were the first to pass through the destruction machine evil had contrived, but she was astonished at being hungry and at eating, she was so poor all of a sudden, it was as if Michel himself hadn't even noticed how dispossessed she was, stripped of everything, even her skin, her heart, and she could feel liquid weakness all around her as she leaned against the banisters, and yet being there felt good, perhaps all victims experienced such moments of remission, threat-free illuminations; perhaps Mozart, as he was about to leave the world and the promises of his genius which was worth so much more than the world he was relinquishing, had listened to *The Magic Flute* with extreme pleasure, thought Florence, perhaps the divine lavishness of his nature weaving its humble way through the deceiving opacity of the world had protected him to the end from our mediocre attacks, perhaps he'd understood that in taking leave of this infernal world he would rid himself forever of the grandiose humiliation that had branded his life, he would no longer have to travel all over Europe, sick and destitute, a beggar before princes, all that would finally cease, deliverance from life would be deliverance from humiliation and from begging, it would be the paradise he had been dreaming of, it would be *The Magic Flute* floating over our miserable human wreckage and the debasing beggary we'd imposed upon the fluidity of the air and the enchantment of sounds, the rest would never come back again: Mozart would finally be free, thought Florence, he would finally arise from death, alone, with no help from men. It was all Mike's for the afternoon: Lucia, Jojo, the restaurant, old bereaved Tim with his red nose and his beer — was it still afternoon or already evening, Florence had lost touch with the weight and consistency of the hours she was living, still immobile against the banisters — for Gloria had told Mike, "Your Mom's gonna give her show at the *Infini*, it's no big thing, just to show her ass, you, my boy, look after the family," and Mike had understood, he'd put his apron back on, coming and going, master of his kingdom and thinking about Gloria, his mother who was sweating, sweating for all at the *Infini du Sexe*, Gloria always called it *Infini*, and Mike, like her other children, would go when he had "reached manhood", "and you'll sure be proud of your mother then, cause she gives a damn good show," *Infini*, *Infini*, it was so close by, just two or three streets away, thought Mike, "real porno twenty-four hours a day," you went there, stretching out or sitting as you pleased in the shadowy nave, it was man's domain and men — refined men, old men, young, slender, or fat men — flocked there, and each indolent spectator, as he let himself slide down the chute of his fantasies, witnessed the dazzling lust of moments he himself had invented in his most libidinous dreams; usually they were passive men, unable to admit their personal lewdness to themselves let alone to their wives or mistresses, and they turned to Gloria and her sisters for reassurance, for these women dared to act out, often even to exorcise, their dreams for them, they personified man's action, his erection, all that seethed unexpressed inside him; their nude choreography gave shape and weight to it all, man's passivity became the terrain of their victory and they pranced over his obscene pleasures, perhaps Gloria too immolated herself for the sake of the *Infini* which belonged to her as much as to her men for they all knew her, even thought they knew her inside out, but they didn't know that all they possessed of Gloria was the envelope of her body, a carnal shell, and that her wantonness was no greater than that of the prostitutes in Lautrec's or Grosz' paintings, they couldn't see that what flowed over their desire, bubbling out to tax or satisfy their hunger, was nothing more than a fleeting conversation between her flesh and theirs that lasted only as long as she was on stage dancing or caressing herself, while within herself she did not adhere to them, she was there only to perform this labour of satiation that they needed from women, she purified them of their hunger, their infinite craving for her, and if they were won over by the smell of her, by her gestures and the erotic scenery that surrounded her, they still didn't know her, didn't know that she in no way submitted as they played laughingly with the stuff of her body, thinking they were inhaling and possessing her; her private truth that they couldn't grasp was a higher truth, who knows, perhaps it was her own *Infini* of which she let them glimpse only occasional flashes, and that part of herself would never belong to them — at least that was the way Judith Lange saw Gloria, as a victim, as another victim of all those paradises we are driven to create in our image; Florence had smiled at Judith with distrust, so that's how you see the world, poor thing, she'd said, you think that purgatory, the purgatory Christians and all those who believe in sacrilege talk about, is nothing more than our earthly paradise, a victims' paradise; can't you see that that too may be utopian, Florence had insisted, has it never occurred to you that there may be no victims, just torturers? an entire people of executioners and torturers? but now, sitting on the stairs staring at the vomit stains on the rug, Florence had misgivings about what she'd said, Mike's tiny, dry, burning hand had taken the dirty plate away, she had wanted to speak to the boy but he was already gone, it was late already, he thought, and why wasn't Lucia home from school yet, why did she arrive later every day, sex, that was the *Infini*, Gloria said, sex, it's a very precious vase, that's how he saw his mother, a fragile coffer, and he was anxious to see her again, she alone knew how to freshen his bandages, they'd go to San Francisco together this summer, summer would be here before long and who was that woman, fiftyish, well dressed but sad, sitting on the stairs, she wasn't a guest like the others, Tim the Irishman, depraved as he was, didn't know she was there, yes, Gloria was a very fragile vase, sex, that was it, thought Mike, it wasn't like they all said, especially Tim and Charlie who were so wicked, it was a fragile vase, and the dishes were piling up in the dim kitchen, if Lucia didn't come home he'd have to go looking for her in the streets, and if Gloria was a fragile vase, a coffer full of secrets, wouldn't all those moles that went creeping after her at the *Infini* damage her in the long run, leave her with some irreparable wound, but in the meantime there were all those dishes to be washed and Jojo whom he felt like slapping was sticking to him like glue, following him everywhere, "Shut up or I'll kill you!" he said. He knew she didn't believe him and yet Jojo's eyes were already wise and dark with premonitions, kill, die, "and how're you gonna kill me?" she asked, "I'll just do what Tim did to his dog," said Mike, "they'll put you to sleep with a needle because you're just a little dog anyway, that way you won't be under my feet any more," Jojo cuddled up closer against Mike's legs, he pushed her off without anger as he would have pushed a puppy away, he himself felt a bit like Tim the dog, stunned, drowsy in the hum of his thoughts, caught up in the pain grinding his forehead, and Florence recalled something else Judith Lange had told her — like all the things Judith Lange said it was strange, the clamours of a world from which reason had been banned, crushed, and it was even more unstable, thought Florence, than the tottering banisters against which she, Florence, was leaning, she who no longer had any real weight in the world unless it was her thoughts that strayed, roaring and precise — Judith had said that even if she knew nothing about Egyptian art, and even less about the tomb-like face of life of which Florence had spoken and which she affirmed was her own although apparently Judith Lange didn't believe her for she went on talking as if she'd always been alive, even forcing the yoke of her first name upon her, Florence, Florence, yes you exist, you are there and I see you, Judith, like so many young people, knew nothing of Egyptian art, thought Florence, yet at Chartres Judith had noticed that life was created not by a woman but by a man, at Chartres they had sculpted only men as givers of life, what do you expect, Florence had replied, the workers of that time

prostrated themselves before the only Creator they'd
known, the builders, all men, construed life according to a
masculine architecture, a masculine projection, and hadn't
Judith told Florence she was lacking in loyalty, but to
what, to whom, and why, Florence asked herself; it
seemed to her that she would perish by that very loyalty,
the weight of her loyalty that represented so little to
others, and Florence thought she would have to go back to
Chartres to understand what Judith had meant, and
wasn't it humiliating to be still a prey to that kind of
curiosity, that instinct that was perhaps our last tie with
the world; Florence pulled her bony knees up against her,
they were so insignificant, just like the rest of her body
that waited on the stairs for who knows what, and then
suddenly there had been a whispering down below, like an
extenuated song, a lullaby maybe that Mike was singing to
his sister in a barely audible voice, he's singing, he's alive,
he proclaims the right to live, thought Florence, listening
to the lullaby that floated up to her, broken by sighs;
instead of slapping Jojo, Mike was slowly putting her to
sleep at his feet while he washed the dishes, with innocu-
ous words whose poignant banality seized Florence's soul,
her thoughts went back to Judith Lange, to the crazy
things Judith had said to her, sometimes in the concentra-
tion camps they spared the lives of those who consented to
bless their own execution and agony with the grace of a
sublime voice, they'd have made Mike, Michel Agneli, wait
a second, an hour at the most, for though the jolty rise and
fall of his voice was touching, even pathetic, it was lacking
that crystalline tone, like clay glazed by sacrificial tears,
that had moved those connoisseurs of calamities — they'd

also been connoisseurs of a music that rose as from the beyond, and of which they were so envious that they believed that they themselves, as they quenched their thirst at the cups running over with blood and lamentations, would become the very melody of Mozart or Strauss that came trickling from throats turned to fountains, that they would inherit the very voices they were smothering, drying up to the bone. And yet the mournful song did Florence good, she was being rocked, yes, it was the rocking of misfortune but Mike's voice caressed the boulders of hate she felt piling up inside her, softened their hardness, and she recalled moments of peace, yes she'd also had peaceful moments but it hurt so much to think that when she had shared them with her husband she hadn't known that the love they'd cultivated together, the love that was their pride and consecration — for, as everybody said of them, few couples loved each other as much as they did — she had had no idea that the consecration of the days they were living together would with time turn into a bellicose affair, an assassin's weapon, she was resting, had she not whiled away her life resting in the shadow of that man while he gathered cold figures into columns, iridescent figures corresponding to the opaline quality of his inventor's mind, she had somehow felt that his power must be formidable since he shared it with no one, and he would say why don't you go out and get some sun, have a good time, you're here for a rest; Italy was beautiful, Italy, and now, sitting on the stairs, she thought yes, life is beautiful when the art of our illusions breeds in our memories all those paintings still charged with light and intoxicating scents; over there she had gone swimming in the Blue Grotto—was not the chain of harmonious sounds she'd heard there in itself the entire sea, the whole blue sky, a painting for our senses, for we have always known how to subdue the violence of our struggle by insisting on the world's beauty, and it was true, after all, the Blue Grotto existed, there existed a sea and a sky that were always blue, that had been so in the thirteenth century as they are today, she had seen them, drunk with gratitude for the beauty of a world whose light declined less rapidly than ours she had observed with a dazzled eye the ruins of a temple, an island covered with olive trees, a Greek amphitheatre or a cathedral, those slopes, those cliffs and orange groves or the apotheosis of sunsets, all these, Florence thought, were the painted ruins of those who could not paint, they were our historical treasures, just as each country, even the most miserable, the most oppressed, could boast of having had its own Jesus Christ or Napoleon, we were weak and passionate about our picturesque treasures, we clung to our Romans and our Greeks and sometimes, if we had really listened to our-selves, thought Florence, we would have thought that we were eternal, that we had settled in for eternity in the walls of our ancient cities, our ancient civilizations, that we would never perish inside our fortifications, our glass citadels; she had thought about all that while she was basking in the sun or swimming in the Blue Grotto, and then Mike had stopped singing, Lucia had just come in and Mike was scolding her, Jojo woke up crying, Mike asked Lucia what she'd been doing and she just stared at him mutely, "and stop chewing gum like that, it's ugly, Mom's still at her show, take your books out of your bag," but he knew she would refuse to study, tonight like the night before she'd refuse, so he kept quiet in his anger and only stared at her, confused, and said nothing. Powerlessness is perhaps the most painful of our worldly abdications, and suddenly Mike felt the pain of it, he understood that Lucia wasn't listening to him and that he had absolutely no power over the stubborn profile that would reveal none of its secrets to him, over that turbulent animal existence that went on alone without him, no power, nor even a hope of tenderness because Lucia, even if she was only a destitute child, had taken possession of herself, of that which was her solitude, her personal power, the power of her own depravation in a depraved society, and if such was her desire he couldn't say anything, no, nothing, he preferred not knowing what she did after school, but Lucia, like Gloria or Jojo, or his father who'd been gunned down in the street by a rival gang, was Mike, all that was his inheritance, his greatness and his humiliation, and deep inside them all he read the story of a mortified greatness, his, that of his brother and sisters, and he knew that nobody on earth would ever understand them, they would die out in the mud or the blood, taking with them the secret on which Lucia's lips, her stubborn profile, were the final seal, those lips, that profile on which Mike's power-lessness fixed itself, and still silent, with the weight of dead anger in him, he went to sit alone by the window and lit a cigarette with a dry trembling hand, the hand that had given Florence the plate of spaghetti in the stairway, this hand, he thought, which would serve neither to protect nor to comfort; it was still nice out and he contemplated the vast red and golden sky, blinking his eyes, extremely

weary all of a sudden, the light fell over him with indo-
lence and tranquillity, Florence was there watching Mike
from a distance but he didn't know it, he'd forgotten her,
he liked that muffled light, he was consumed in it and all
Florence perceived of him was a stoical figure that was no
longer the Mike whose feelings of revolt and rage had yet
to be reined in, no, it was another of those faces that had
spoken to her alone in museums, a portrait Munch had
painted of his ailing sister sitting like that at a window,
when outside it might have been spring or the translucent
invitation of nothingness, our gaze caught in all its fragility
at a window — it was Mike, his bandages like a white tiara
on his head, and just as Munch had begun the portrait of
his dying sister several times, imploring life with violent
jabs of charcoal, pencil, and brush, perhaps even making
fun of that powerlessness which characterizes us all, even
the creator in his greatest moments of creation, of liberation, dreaming of casting the features on his canvas with a
stroke of the palette knife in the same way the light of the
red, indolent sky moulded and hollowed out this unflinch-
ing model that was Mike's face; one would have thought
him untouched by the light working over him, he gazed
into the distance, inviolable in his misfortune and imperious in the silence he seemed to exhale and Florence
remained still, for it would have been terrible to upset his
quiet stupor. Art undoubtedly surpassed our most doleful
tragedies, thought Florence; even if the face depicted by
Munch was only a vague memory — if you recalled it at all
— you couldn't forget the essence of what he'd revealed
on canvas, the melancholy curve of a child's profile whose
face would never again turn towards us, the dull light of

the pale eyes, the emaciated triangle of the fever-ridden cheeks and chin, right down to a detail that now seemed to relive itself in all the fullness of art within Mike's features though nobody would have thought to sketch Mike's profile, yes, a detail the painter had taken such pains to render, the fine thinness of the hair, the frittering away of what had been a head of hair on the bared skull that once had been covered with supple locks caressed by the wind, filtered and untangled by light, it had all been shed and scattered already, none of it existed any more, or at least Florence foreshadowed its disappearance beneath the white cloth wound around Mike's forehead and she thought no, my God, I can't resign myself to that, no, and the rosy complexion, no, no she wouldn't resign herself to that; but it wasn't only the veil of white, innocent death that Florence mistrusted so in her dreams and that would soon descend on Mike's eyelids, there was — and it had nothing to do with beauty or art — an abject, arrogant whiteness, a whiteness she'd recognized as her own while leafing through a magazine in her lawyer's office or in another of the empty places she'd filled with her absence, casting glances from one wall to the other like balls that had lost their bounce, waiting for a solution to her destiny, yes, that heavy whiteness, contemptible but inspiring no contempt for itself in itself, the white man walked along the streets of Madras, businessman, tourist or vacationer, he was there, blinding everything around him with his dull whiteness, blind himself behind his dark glasses, just walking and then there was something at his feet, he couldn't back away from it in the crowd, a package flayed by so many feet, so much indifference, a baby wrapped in a rag—sometimes they didn't even have a stitch of a rag on them—a naked thing lying there, living detritus, and they all came and went, you could see them filing by day after day, you could even see them in vulgar magazine pictures, unmoved by the ball of life that hunger or abandonment had accidentally thrown down at their feet, it was as though the streets and sidewalks that had witnessed man's trampling for centuries absorbed life swathed in a rag just as they had drunk up dust, sperm, or blood, all these macabre essences were alike, they reduced the human race to what it was for its progenitors, and you could no longer be moved, no, you no longer could, and Florence reflected that Dostoevsky had been right when he'd defined man as being at the same time sentimental and wicked, for he was all that at once, he recoiled from the starving thing that whimpered at his feet, for it was just a piece of filth even if it was still crying and breathing, there were deadly germs beneath that just-born filth, an obscene stench, you couldn't take it home to your own house and after all millions of them were found lying in our city streets, our countries, every day, avoiding it was above all a matter of hygiene; but man was sentimental too—for you could become attached, let yourself be moved by the small body when it was your own offspring, the issue of a clean body, of your brilliant, purified sperm, and in such cases the woman's body became the temple of a ghost that you called my light, my plenitude, it was a part of yourself and no threat, that's exactly how you created a race, a hair colour, the colour of your own skin, a family, a country, and the clean white being who emerged from this temple would be loved and respected, he would be the prince of

our world, the child-king, it didn't shock us, thought
Florence, we weren't even upset by this tiny package of
lamentations we were about to push away with our
leather-bound, iron-studded feet, with our silken heels, in
the streets of Madras or elsewhere, no, strangely, our
maternal conscience, our paternal righteousness was perfectly at peace, for we were, first and foremost, father or
mother of our own self, and these rags at our feet cried and
complained in a tongue that was strange to us, we went
on, deaf to these cries, went on, thought Florence, stirred
by the treacherous voice that rose from our entrails and
thinking my light, my plenitude, oh, how lovely it all was,
and the ties of blood were so strong, Judith Lange had
explained to Florence, that even if honest parents had
been known to disown a son who had become a thief or a
daughter who had become a prostitute as if they were
surreptitious grafts on their own solid morality, in the
course of history many children of great criminals had also
been known to defend their parents' crimes, venerating,
far more than the blood that had been shed, the first kiss
they'd received on the forehead, all the dreams of which
they'd afterwards been stripped; they remembered the
fond father they'd had as tiny children, the kind paternal
figure leaning over the crib, and when they were confronted later on with men who had been hanged for their
crimes or driven to suicide in prison cells in order to avoid
worldwide condemnation, they refused that part of the
evidence, it wasn't their father but a victim of duty, a
victim of history, and they couldn't understand, no they
couldn't understand, they were shown figures, mountains
of corpses and they didn't know what people were talking

about; if only everyone had forgotten about them, but no, they were there, they had survived, and even today they constantly beheld, over and above the walls of crime, the supreme authority of a father who had won their confidence by his gentleness and charm; this same man couldn't possibly have strangled thousands of small children, it was all in people's imaginations, it had to be buried away in the cellar of history, no, the man they'd known had been a good father, a sentimental father, such a good father that they had preserved, in the name of a past however bad, those things that at least could not be rubbed out — his armchair, the philosophy book he used to read before falling asleep at night — and even these daughters and sons of a cursed heredity had a right to such tender sentiments, and who would have thought to rob them of their heart-rending memories even if that same adored father had suddenly one day been accused of all the crimes of the earth and arraigned, judged, and hanged? Florence, watching Mike sitting at the window, fell to daydreaming in turn, fell into her own drowsiness, it suddenly seemed to her that her existence was also giving in, slowing down, yielding to a consciousness that was no longer present but keeping watch in the distance, a consciousness that had dozed off perhaps; then she closed her eyes and began to dream but her dreams raced around her like whirlwinds, and like needles of consciousness they lacerated the flesh even while consciousness seemed to rest, there was someone there, a beggar perhaps but she couldn't tell who exactly, it was someone who seemed to live in a hole of shadows and she couldn't see his head, but it was something swarming close by her, and a hand born from an invisible monstrosity caught hers, a voice said, "Come down, come down with me," it was like a host of caresses swarming over her, and all these brushings of a hand and a mouth that had sprung up from the secretions of the shadow, from the sombre ravine of her own violence, maybe, for our dreams are also of our making, horrified her and she woke with a start, Mike was standing before her, tugging at her arm, "I've brought you some coffee, my mother's back from her show, drink it while it's hot"; he looked at her defiantly, a hand in his pocket, and she heard him say, "Come on, drink it, why are you looking at me like that?" Mike waited, staring at her, "Mommy says it'll perk you up . . ." and she couldn't explain how each drop of the coffee pained her as it slid down her throat, she felt oppressed, subjugated by this guard who exercised his will upon her, and she missed the days in which a cup of coffee or a glass of liquor, rather than bending her body to the constraint of pain, had distracted her, given her a lift, but the coffee was strong, drops of fire bringing her back to life, cheering her, in spite of everything, in her sadness, and she smiled at Mike who continued to stare at her with the grave eyes of a watchman, she wondered if this look would follow her to the other side of life, and what would he tell his mother when he saw that respectable woman, Florence, Florence Gray — for her tranquil inquisitor had understood that she wasn't like him, like any of them, that she wasn't one of those meant to be looted and massacred at dawn or during those hours of the night when even the police dogs pretended to be asleep behind the barbed wire of the yard — yes, what would he say to his mother, Gloria, when he discovered this woman who had decided upon her own capitulation, her own undoing, dangling on the end of a rope, of a scarf, of a stocking perhaps that she'd knotted around her neck, a woman of whom nothing remained but a pile of fears? Yes, thought Florence, nothing but the shreds of fear we leave behind along with the mislaid, rejected body, the stigmata of our fear, a deluge of sweat, tears, or blood — would it not be scandalous to leave this corpse behind, the body still quivering with fear and giving off pestilential odours, reeking of the sudden decomposition set off by the fear we hold within ourselves our whole lives long? Florence had also dreamed, a dream that had lasted no longer than a breath as she let herself slide down against the banisters, that she was going back to her deserted apartment — what we call deserted, she thought, is the emptiness created by absence, separation, death, in her dream she'd rediscovered her apartment, her furniture, her collection of paintings, all the pillars of her former existence which had suddenly collapsed, leaving only faint traces, so much dust; she saw a painting that had formerly conjured up for her the light, even the smell of the sea against the background of a Mediterranean sky, a sky whose vast blueness was broken just by the tip of a white cloud, a blue, distant, uniform sky which seemed, however, set there as it was against emptiness, to be made of a penetrable matter, there was nothing cruel about it, nothing more than the indifference of blue matter inviting you to penetrate it, and you looked up and your skyward glance drifted off and lost itself like everything that navigates in space, but in her dream the painting was blank, the Mediterranean sky that had been painted in oils was no longer there, you could see that the light must have been dazzlingly intense, something of its essence remained while the characters that had been like specks of colour at the edge of the canvas, as humble and charming as flowers between the sea and the sky, had gone else-where, all that remained was the empty frame and its rectangular sharpness, and Florence wandered, wandered against the blind, luminous surface, she had spent so much time there, sitting in her armchairs or lazing away Sundays on the sofa, surrounded by books and newspapers — each one of these familiar objects had assumed, at one moment or another, its particular seductive or appeasing role in her life, each bore the mark of her passage in this place, and yet the armchair was empty, here and there patches of light on the furniture seemed to indicate that somebody had been present only seconds before; the walls had once been covered with a forest of souvenirs, pictures of her hus-band, of her son, but none of it existed any more; empti-ness, emptiness everywhere, thought Florence, and then she woke and realized that her watch had stopped, it was still pointing to 11:45 A.M., she shook her wrist and extended her hand but there was no life left in the tiny silver case, nothing would set it in movement again and neither would the painter's canvas recover the sea or the sky; knowing that gave you a kind of serenity, knowing that the objects had ceased feeling and so had ceased suffering, knowing that so many defenceless things were no longer in contact with life's shocks, its drama and harshness, nobody would come to buy, conquer, or steal them, no, in accordance with a secret order they would file into the tomb of the person who had cherished them in her lifetime, thought Florence, but as she contemplated her watch, now just a dead eye gaping into nothingness, she grieved for the object that was leaving the world before her, just as she had grieved, during her dream-visit to her apartment, for the touching smile of her son at three years old, for the delicate features that time would alter either by thickening them enough to fit a virile mask, or by effacing them with a smug expression and adolescent presumptions. Florence's mind turned to captivity, to the feeling of entrapment that always managed to annihilate us; we were, she thought, horribly diminished, defeated by living conditions that allowed us no promises, no hope of lesser misfortunes; she contemplated her watch and this dead, already memoryless time that was soon going to bury her days, her hours — she couldn't even touch the atom of life which had fled without warning from something as familiar as a watch, this toy that led us wherever it chose, this object so closely bound to our most intimate pulsations yet made of matter as indifferent as the painting of which she'd dreamed, this matter that became an adversary by its very indifference to the difficulty we experienced just trying to live, but all these things, like so many similar, indifferent objects, continued to lead their seemingly fleshly, durable, energetic existences around her, all of them, even Tim without his dog for he'd now set his lusty old heart on Gloria, Gloria and Lucia, one day he would be master of Lucia's erotic fragility, he thought, Gloria, Lucia, he looked at them, sensual and happy, for the beast in him was panting once again, Gloria, Lucia, listless hopes alternating in his mind, and unlike the Ireland of his memories they could be attained, devoured, he had only to touch Lucia's fresh little face with his lazy paw; she was already so arrogant and cutting, just like the woman, like Gloria, her laugh was so sneaky, Gloria pushed her daughter off with an impatient gesture, saying, "Go do your homework with Mike now," but Lucia clasped her mother in her arms, "Well, you can at least help me wait on the clients, then," and Mike took it all in, he was frightened, captive, there was no longer any way to flee, Florence thought, no, he no longer could, it was too late, he was part of the world and once you were part of the world you couldn't dream, you were far from the transcending womb of dreams and like it or not you had to brave the stinging arrows of pain that came flying towards you, for the cage shut around you at your very awakening, at birth, and it wouldn't open for a long time after that and even when it did it would only be to reveal a black grating, a still deeper mourning, and Lucia's fingers were toying with old Tim's hair, it made Mike want to beat her up, it was nothing, hardly a gesture, he wasn't even sure of it but he would have beaten her, beaten her for he was captive, immobile and captive, and his dream, or what was left of it, had become so tenuous that he scarcely believed it any more, San Francisco, yes, Gloria and the blazing sun that would consume the ashes of his bones, or else another dream, oh, how did one dream, he no longer knew how, in the cruelty of that instant all his hopes were about to turn against him — his mother, Lucia, old Tim, and all that he called his life, life killed and robbed, it hurtled the muted, blind light he so dreaded at him; Florence felt sorry for him but it was dead pity since neither Mike nor herself would come out of it alive, she thought, walk out of the space they were shut up in, both of them so majestically calm that if a stranger had entered this place where people laughed and had fun, drank and fornicated, he would have been completely unaware of the quiet death-rattle that passed from one dying person to the other. But all men possessed another dream, a hidden, impenitent dream that perhaps lingered in their hearts a long time after they'd left this world, surely men went on dreaming, and this desire to dream had already transfigured Mike, Mike and Florence, although Florence no longer hoped for that transfiguration of love which touched Mike's pale smile from time to time; after all there was still, at least in Mike's case, the hope of finding love and reassurance in a world that promised no gentleness, governed as it was by the sole laws of violence, and yet in his weakness, in his gentleness, he kept hoping, believing; Florence turned her sad eyes from him, unwilling to be witness to that hope, no, and Mike who was just a child, a broken stem, part of the same incomplete hope that his smile revealed so perfectly — for hope, like pain, has engraved its revealing, visibly indecent symptoms in each of us — and wasn't Mike at that moment, for Florence, one of those plaintive faces, silent but plaintive, indecent with truth, that she was there just to contemplate, to receive; but she, who already felt the silent chill of death against her bones, could no longer receive or understand that silken, transparent flesh, so vulnerable still that it made her tremble, and she pushed Mike's face away without a cry or a gesture, repeating to herself, my God, oh my God, what on earth is he thinking about? Mike's sharp but weary, so weary eye penetrated a world he had judged febrile and deceiving, his mother, Tim, Lucia, and the whole howling mass teeming around them, that's what living was, he seemed to reflect, and he told himself that truth, or reality, was not to be found there, maybe there was a world somewhere far away from them all, completely removed from their weaknesses and their quarrels, all those uglinesses they had indulged and enjoyed, surely there was another world, he would appease his heart's longings there, and so he dreamed and his dream carried him gently away, far from them all, he followed Tim's dog and the miraculous swarm of victims towards a paradise inhabited neither by God nor by angels; it was his, it was the survivors' long pilgrimage towards the light, and Tim the dog was there, far from them all, and the unknown boy whose picture had been in the morning papers, he had set fire to his clothes in the street and had suffered burns "over only 40 per cent of his body", they'd written, well, 40 per cent was a lot and it wasn't enough to kill you, and you lay there between sky and earth, even if you were still blazing with a monstrous anger you didn't cry out, you died slowly, and the survivors' paradise was far off in the distance, the rays of its cold golden sky came towards you, licked your feet, your carbonized hands and Florence had seen Gloria approach Mike in the evening light and draw his head to her bosom, "Come on, boy, why don't you get some sleep," she murmured, growling like a beast, for she moaned for the child who no longer heard her, then said, "Listen, Mike, we're gonna take off pretty soon, listen, we're gonna take off for San Francisco, we'll go even farther than that, yeah, it's always light and warm there, and it's so far away, so far away that even the dust has a name, it's a dry, dainty dust, listen Mike, listen," Gloria was saying to her son, yes they'd soon go far away, towards a wonderfully arid land, already the motorcycle was carrying them off on its winged flight in the sun, they passed a river, an ocean, leaving the cities and their thick clouds of dirt behind, you hear, Mike, yes, he was listening, but did the survivors forgive, Mike wondered, did Tim the dog forgive, there had been the other desert-like immensity Florence had seen from her miserable room, the one from which there was no return for it was too cold and nothing grew there, and then there was Mike's desert, the one he crossed with Gloria, a mauve oasis full of flowers, covered with dry, dainty dust that scorched you as you passed, and when you woke up in the morning "in a campground as big as heaven on earth," Gloria said, you were struck by the shrill din of the birds, the lemon trees were full of them, suddenly a huge, dense vegetation smothered you with its fragrances, with its cries, and you lay still on your back and gazed at the unchanging sky, stunned by the fragrance of lavender, you didn't dare move, and Gloria's hand was resting lightly on Mike's forehead, in this moment of indolent musing, thought Florence, Gloria brought to mind a Madonna painted by Munch, a red apparition whose shape was magnified so against a black wall of night that it was hard to tell whether the painter's model was meant to be a woman of pleasure or a valiant, unmysterious Virgin spilling around her, with the abandon of her dark-ringed eyes and fleshy lips, the avidness of her desire to protect, her eager tenderness; but Mike was swathed in Gloria's indulgence towards men, nourished by her perfumes and, perfectly still under the caress of her fingers, he confidently inhaled that aroma of the wild vegetation surrounding him, it was like being in the middle of a garden, Gloria was saying that the days would be endless there, the blinding light of the sky never abandoned you, and when you went to sleep it was without effort or dreams, for dreams are for those who live and breathe; the birds might be singing a mocking song in the emptiness of the dry, flamboyant evening that would never darken into night, but Florence, like Mike, had seen the page of the newspaper — the boy who had put an end to just 40 per cent of his life, but why, she asked herself, wondering if Judith Lange was at his bedside, that bedside that would mean still being there the day after, surviving the fire, the derisive permanence of sacrifice attaching itself to him tomorrow and the day after tomorrow and what did Judith Lange think of all that; fragrances of lavender and lemon trees wafted towards Mike but there was also an odour of fire and decomposition, he was a soldier, a deserter, a wanderer and there was a chance that Judith Lange was at his bedside, thought Florence, for she was the friend of suicides and this one had come from another country, not long before they'd praised the beauty of his generation, called him a flower child, and he was going to perish in flames; who could have imagined, seeing what a beautiful baby he had been at birth, that at the dawn of his life his fathers would send him off to massacre innocent people, to loot and kill like the worst assassins, he who'd been born in a crib of abundance had become a child of shame, his grace and beauty had betrayed him, for he had killed, set fire to villages, shed blood, this flower child, and he hadn't been able to understand why, when he was still so young, they were initiating him into the art of villainy, giving him a taste for murder, no, he hadn't understood, nor why on earth he should survive, by what irony of misfortune, who knows, Florence reflected, perhaps Judith Lange, at the exiled boy's bedside in some depressing asylum, was laying a cool hand on his forehead, yes, all of it could very well be true, we could accept it since the cup of our life contained all these horrors, and while the light of an oasis, the peace of the desert, penetrated Mike's heart, Florence recalled a whole series of luminous days that had kept her captive in this world at a time when she'd played at living serenely by her husband's side, following him everywhere, on streets, on beaches, stretching her life out beside him as one lies down in a tomb, so close, so close that she could barely breathe, who knows, maybe it was happiness that was suffocating her in the solemn, gigantic embrace whose sudden loss had crushed, annihilated her like a stream of lava gushing over sandy dunes, she had known she was alive, that someone was there, and from now on that side of her life was a gaping hole, it had been pulverized to blood-stained particles of dust, never again would he return, take up the place that had been his; she brushed her ankle with the tip of her fingers, he'd left his mark there one day, they'd been dozing side by side in lounge chairs, captives of the inexorable light spilling from the blue Mediterranean sky, and she had felt the imprint of an imperious foot on her bare, slim ankle, one toe especially stroking her ankle tranquilly, it was he, his presence there, and hesitant, she'd felt her body soar with desire, perhaps everyone had noticed, even the pathetic swimmers in the pool, how could she deceive them in such an unswerving light, how could she lie to them when her husband's gesture was so dazzlingly sincere, she'd been captive, yes, and accomplice too as she'd turned to smile at him, there it was for all to see; she belonged to him, she had yielded all her resistance to him, and now she was sitting on the stairs remembering the possessive stroke of that caress, and now she thought she heard a moaning close by, one of the doors was ajar, somebody was being tortured there, in the hotel, it was coming from the second floor, yes, she rose, approached and saw an elderly man thrashing a boy of about twenty, she wanted to ask why but the old man was already speaking to her, his voice was that of a sensitive man, a professor maybe, he was still wearing his beret and his tweed overcoat, he pointed at his tormented angel — it was hard to tell, thought Florence, which of the two was making the other suffer more — and said in a kindly voice, "What can be done, madame, it's the only thing that excites him and he's crazy about it. . . ." Florence saw it all like a dream and yet the tortured boy turned an imploring face to her, a face that was touched from time to time by an ecstatic smile; it was as though the fine body, naked and pale, marked by blows and injuries, was offering itself up in spite of the heavy chains, calling this mysterious martyr-dom upon itself, and yet for Florence it was all like a dream for this body, this face that was being conscientiously covered with racking blows, also represented one of the faces of love, an embodiment of love, thought Florence, for passion made you dream of closing in upon your prey this way, keeping the object of your passion in your clutches; perhaps the professor in the tweed coat was simply the servant of a dream, perhaps with time and the assiduous practice of pederasty he had come to realize his most secret dreams and now he kept his prisoner shut up in this room; others had longed to be dictators, to rule over the entire world, but the only power a solitary man could hope for was ruling over a being still lonelier than himself, and once this prisoner had been chosen, once he'd entered the ritual space of the room he rarely left it, they came up to feed him, cajole him, punish or please him, and he no longer had to walk the streets where it seemed to him a masterless, unpossessed crowd roamed and fluttered around aimlessly, in vain; he now lived according to monastic rites, day after day his jailer came to visit him and dress his wounds until time no longer existed for him, until he felt himself dissolve in a passive eternity of pleasure from which he had no desire to return, not even just for a moment to breathe the unbreatheable air outside; and Florence saw Lucia pass hurriedly by her, Lucia who asked the professor and the boy, with an arrogant look, if they were hungry, then flew downstairs without bothering to wait for an answer, gay and light, unknowingly flouting her brother's dignity; he saw her movements as the dance of a young being who'd already left scruples and candour behind, and knew he wouldn't have time to defend her against the iniquities of life; he told her to open her books on the table but she paid no heed; if it was true, as Gloria said, pressing her son's aching head to her breast, that you could live on honey and fruit in the desert, if it was still true, the sight of Lucia on the stairs made Mike forget it; he saw her approach almost imperceptibly, like a kind of poignant, insolent evil that was not only out of his reach but that he had to treat gently even if something inside him was already mourning for her soul; Florence, though a stranger, knew how mortified he felt, but she seemed too weary to speak, perhaps she was a cold woman, a woman of another race, she was haughty and inaccessible, she'd left the world of the living and all that could still be recognized of her was this rigid apparition in an empty hall; the newspaper had called the boy who had suffered burns over 40 percent of his body a "drop-out", drop-out, Gloria repeated, yesterday he'd been a flower child but a flower of the night, a drop-out, and yet his was a pious generation who took to ecstasy, once they had cast off their war uniforms and set their weapons aside they could go home, kneel down, and pray to the sun, yes, said Gloria, all that was also true, they fell on their knees before a spring and mumbled their gratitude for the trickle of water as yet untouched by the pollution of the cities; they were going to take it all in, God, the sun, the spring that was still pure, they'd go to the ends of the earth in search of it all, to far-off countries where faith still burned strong, for you had to pray and believe and not die, you told yourself that God must be hiding out somewhere, it might even be beneath the stony surface of Saharan deserts; and then there was also the possibility that He was present everywhere, in the sad circle of the nightly moon, for example, but when you were young and handsome you preferred begging a bit of warmth from the sun, for the sun was voluptuousness, youth, triumph, it was joy-bait, and Mike thought about his older sister who'd left home a long time ago already, his mother said she'd disowned her own family, Berthe, he thought, Berthe Agneli, maybe he'd never see her again, Berthe didn't like them for she thought they were all condemned, they had the plague, no, she'd never see them again, she was so much better off where she was, in the fortress of the university; once she'd passed her exams she would crush them all, she was in the library, it was a safe place and she went there every day to study, never running around like the other girls her age, all they ever thought about was going out and having a good time, Berthe studied all the time, preparing for her diploma, once she'd graduated she would be free and all her clients would be rich, never would she plead the cause of these villainous minor criminals who fouled the world with their petty, bungled crimes — they didn't even know how to kill in style, they were all abject, her father, her uncles, tomorrow her brothers, her mother Gloria; but she was safe now, sheltered by the glass-walled library, she could be seen bending over her books, yes, her slender silhouette could be glimpsed through the slits in the shelves, perhaps, even here there was too much light and transparency, sometimes she was afraid, but it was nothing compared to her terrorized past; completely removed from them all she'd acquired a new dignity, she was rigid and pure and she loved nobody, neither men nor women nor the students, she spent her time going back and forth between her boarding-house and the university, so severe that she attracted nothing more than the cold waves one usually sensed only in uninhabited places; the only feeling that still gravitated around her was that rising coldness, a rising rage, it was a barren, wasted kind of feeling and it suited her fine, sometimes she was afraid, yes, especially when she had to walk in the city, to go into dark bookstores in search of a book she needed for her research, she went with the fear of seeing some dangerously familiar figure suddenly rise up before her as if emerging from the dense servility of life itself; but she was protected here on this academic island where you dedicated yourself completely to studies, nobody knew who she was, no criminals came here, each person lived according to an order, a hierarchy, the stain of the paternal blood faded away and she was just a face among others, but behind it all there was rage, the rage to pass her examinations, to lift herself up and melt into the flock of the strong; she was small and slim but she had the persistence of insects building a wall; so much hateful, silent rage, the obstinate will to learn, to conquer, to vanquish them all, wore on the nerves but she'd made it, she wasn't like the rest of them, devastated, destroyed before their time, she wasn't like her brother, Mike, Michel Agneli, that doomed brother who'd been the only decent being in her perverted lineage, and who was going to perish for all the others. And then Mike had forgotten Berthe's existence, it flowed along far from all of them, it was elsewhere, in a distant place, and other dreams came beading off Gloria's cool fingers, it was during the night, perhaps, he tossed and turned with pain, rolling from one side to the other and trying not to wake his brother Luigi, he was running with his mother in those regions of the desert where dwarf roses flower in the chaos of the dunes, they seem to keep the secret of their survival to themselves, so much so, thought Mike, that they'll resist man's destruction and one day, when mortals have killed each other off, these roses will become the resurrection of the desert, of the sand that has nurtured them, they'll still be there with their fragrant perfume — Mike had dreamed that he was running with Gloria and suddenly they had come across a book abandoned in the sand, "Wait, Mom," he said to Gloria, "I want to read it to you," and she waited, immense and generous as she stood before him in the sun; there was no shadow between them now, the Hôtel des Voyageurs was closed, no shadow at all, not even Tim's breath, not even the memory of his step, just the sun and yet, in spite of the sun and the blue sky, a storm wind arose without warning, bearing down on them unexpectedly, violent and wicked; it was a freezing wind or else that summer gust that precedes tornadoes, nature's calamities, suddenly it blew all the pages of the book away, it was a wind that slowed Gloria's pace, her breath, and Mike woke up and Luigi 2, who was as tough or as weak, or both, as his father had been, shoved Mike against the wall saying, "If you don't keep still I'll go get the dogs in the yard...." Mike stopped tossing and the pain in his head snuggled against him — when he was quiet it had a warm, kindly place of its own in him — it was night and the five police dogs were howling in the yard, or else they were silent, a furious drool oozing between their fangs, I'll be a killer too, Luigi 2 had declared, planting his knife in the table, and Gloria had looked at him with astonishment, "Just hold your horses, you're hardly out of diapers yet," but perhaps she was pleased after all with her son's treacherous virility, for she'd smiled, Luigi would be a fine man, hard as a rock, even if you were contemptible it was better to survive than not, survival was the only law human beings obeyed, Lucia was now sitting at the bottom of the stairs scribbling in a notebook and Mike refrained from asking her any more questions, he had no way of knowing what she was thinking about, from time to time she stretched and yawned with a languorous look but all Mike saw out of the corner of his eye was the frayed edge of her blue jeans, no, he no longer saw her, or hardly ever saw her any more, Lucia spent most of her time with her friends, especially with John, her favourite, who was sixteen and often waited for her on Crescent Street; he had a way of spotting clients immediately and he liked acid, he'd tell her in English, *"Go with him, fine..."* or "It's not so much for that as for the speed," John hardly belonged to this world, flipped out already they said, and yet he somehow managed, Lucia couldn't understand how, to get up in the morning, he washed and dressed as in a dream, they brought him his "coke and the LSD" together and it enabled him to arrive at the street corner smiling all over, sniffing the wind, and he was so polite, always so well dressed, that nobody would have guessed; John's father was a dentist and when John went home he was bored, he would ask for a bit of money and then go back out into the street, the street was Lucia and the others, and Lucia scribbled away in her notebook for Michel might still ask her, yes, once again, why she'd been coming in so late and maybe she'd blush, telling lies bothered her, Gloria had told her you can do whatever you want but don't ever lie to your mother, the money came in handy, it was a question of not thinking about it now, and Gloria told Lucia about when she used to visit Charlie in prison on Sundays, Charlie was an ordinary crook with no special qualities, he didn't even know how to make love, Gloria said, but on Sundays sometimes you saw respectable people going to visit their sons, their lovers, their brothers in prison, they weren't all repugnant and banal like Charlie, "Some of them are like princes, with class and polish, you know...." There was one woman who'd had four children, all well brought up, said Gloria, and nobody knew her story, she'd moved away from her own city, had left her friends, her neighbours behind and she too went to the prison on Sundays to see her son, "not a bad boy at all, he was handsome, gentle, with excellent manners...." "And what did he do, Mom?" asked Lucia, and Gloria replied, "They slapped a rape charge on him: a little girl, five years old, murdered in the woods...but none of it's true, the police invent crimes, who wants to sleep with a five-year-old in this day and age? We're not in the Middle Ages, and the guy I'm talking about wasn't a bad type at all, Lucia, worth my Charlie a hundred times over!" Gloria went on talking, telling her story, and Lucia's soul sailed along on her words, on her slightly raucous voice, Gloria, her mother, was right, all the others were wrong, even Mike who'd never have a stereo or plushy rugs in his house, so soft under your feet in winter when it was cold, sometimes he asked almost nothing of them, just that they take off their jeans, so why condemn her for that, why, and Mike asked her what she was drawing, was it Tim's dog, yes it's Tim's dog, and Tim the man said, in tears, he was my dog, I wanted to take him to Ireland with me, and Tim went on crying; now that the only witness of his life was gone, nobody would be able to tell him how he'd lived, no, his earthly life terminated with the end of Tim the dog's reign, in an asylum or a pound, and the memories that had woven his existence together, now that he thought about it, had been just as humble as his dog's life; his country's sea, the brick orphanage, none of it would ever come back now that Tim the dog — lover and beloved — would never again be at his side to remind him, Tim the man, how fragile his hopes were. Florence observed them all: Lucia, Mike, Gloria, Tim and the shadow of his dog, and she said to herself, how did I go on so long without knowing anything about them, ignoring their presence here, forgetting them? For years and years she'd lived without the slightest intuition of the infernal cycle of their suffering or their needs around her, she'd gone on living serenely, shut up neatly in her opaque indifference, serene, yes, for the others hadn't existed, close by or far away they'd had no reality, she'd had no idea that they were all there, breathing in the darkness, and then suddenly she found herself captive of the light of consciousness and it denounced her, no, she wouldn't die before recognizing them all within this infernal circle she'd ignored and scorned until now, what would become of them when she was no longer there — but perhaps not all of them had obstinately probed their painful destiny as she herself did, they didn't have time to resent the certainty she contemplated, that lay before her like a field of sparkling snow on a granite mountain; that certainty, death; she wandered alone, no doubt about it; they were simple people, they had their sorrows but they also had their joys and their hidden destinies, the light didn't reach them — if God existed he had moved so far away that his presence no longer weighed them down, and that was all she could wish for them, that the burden of their misfortunes no longer weigh upon them, and suddenly she noticed that Gloria had overturned a chair in the kitchen in a moment of distraction; Gloria herself had observed the clumsiness of her gesture, but strangely — it was some desperate sign of her unthinking nature that nothing could penetrate — she had made no move to right the chair but had looked at it with scorn, as if trusting it to the uncouthness of her unspoken despair, and the chair, victim of her unjust anger, did not complain, it only spoke, silently, in its abasement, of Gloria; at the same moment Florence remembered another woman, a black woman who'd inadvertently dropped a bar of soap in a drug-store in New York, she too had contemplated the dull, contrite object with irritation, without picking it up, for any desire to undo these frequent gestures of despair was useless; they fell, heavy and forgotten, into the valley of nothingness and the immense confusion of daily life eradicated their traces; but Florence now felt that they left an appalling imprint, even in herself, Florence, who had so often been an indifferent, cool woman; the soap, the chair shattered the silence, the very objects cried and moaned but it was only once you had become an incarcerated soul like Florence that you heard, close by, these hostile whimperings, these cries of protest or weariness, the weariness that made you abandon them there when an exhausted hand, a worn-out body, was suddenly lacking strength to lend them a longer life, for the person who rejected these things destroyed the objects and himself by his resignation. All of us, thought Florence, cherish the hope that nature will make us feel understood, that it will reassure and comfort us; when anguish produces a void, nature is there to fill and fecundate it, and so it was that Mike, whose life was slowly ebbing from his body, lifted himself up from the bowels of the earth, from the dead earth that they wanted to cover him with, to breathe in the fragrant desert air, to listen to palm trees trembling in the evening breeze and nature's trembling clamour triumphing over all the rest; once again Mike saw his sister playing in the park, saw the new grass, dense and yellow, peeping through mounds of grey snow; like Jojo he wanted to relish these first moments of spring when the humidity of winter storms still lingered on, when the earth gave off heady odours that rose like a single bouquet of exhilaration; it was not yet the inebriation of summer days but rather the resurfacing of a craving for life; a pale sun had lit up the city with its cold rays during the harsh winter months, but its light retired early as though it had no real intention of warming you, as though it were only the hint of a sovereign light to come whose warmth trickled through feebly, with parsimonious cruelty; but suddenly the sky opened up in a flood of light and warmth to which you were no longer accustomed and you suspended your life, set aside this finicky existence full of exhaustion and aimless combats and looked to the brilliant sky, the lofty, spellbinding roof whose existence had been forgotten for such a long time; and so Mike lifted himself up from the bowels of the earth thinking, I'm alive, I'm alive, listen to me, me too, like the birds, the mud, the grass, I'm breathing beneath this generous sky, and Florence thought that Mike was just deluding himself again, for nature in no way belonged to him, unless you counted the park where the rich walked their dogs, with its grass, its hundred-year-old tree, its squirrels; yes, you might say the park belonged to him; but as for nature, Florence reflected, it belonged to her, to people like her who'd been born into all the privileges of the earth, but Mike had no way of knowing that thousands of people lived as in another world, Florence's world, a world in which nobody had to suffer from cold or snow; that there was a whole race of human beings who could choose to live permanently in an ecstatic climate with blue skies, warm sun, grass more tender than any he'd ever seen; such people didn't dream of the desert, they had the desert to themselves, they didn't dream of the sea, it was right there lapping their toes in the morning; but you couldn't expect Mike to imagine that kind of life, or if he could imagine it he would see it not as a human possibility but rather as the life of gods; and yet these very gods were his kin, his brothers, they rose with immaculate gestures every morning in the regal whiteness of their own civilization, they could be seen early in the day, dressed in white, browning themselves in the sun, deepening the tan on skin already gilded by all the spring seasons they'd assimilated too quickly beneath their heavenly sky; it all unfolded itself day after day for their exclusive pleasure: the clear sky, the lavish radiance of the sun whose rays they would have liked to keep all for themselves, but apparently you couldn't keep anything for yourself because all of a sudden a noonday breeze, a bit too strong, would get up to remind you that you weren't in a glass cage but right on earth, this place where air and light were only passing by. Florence knew all about it, for once she too had called that golden tan, that freshness, that glaring luminosity her own — or rather she and her husband had called it theirs — and the memory of it all was still clear in her mind: they'd lived a magical life, like all those who partook of their world, passing from one idyllic moment to the next, and in the end their pastoral tale had become a terrible story for it had an ending; what had become of the natural beauty they had adored as much as they had adored themselves? — perhaps, she thought, it was now the scene of a bloody hunt, perhaps they were killing a magnificent wild creature, they were killing everything; all of a sudden the desert bore a likeness to those who had conquered and subjugated it, and chased the contented animal from its domain — you no longer saw the creature bounding from its retreat or quenching its thirst at the pond in the calm of the evening; somehow it had managed to survive, but with a foreboding of its inevitable extinction, like man it was bitter now, it had lost its grace and spontaneity and had been deprived above all of the dignity that only a short time before had been the glory of its kind, and all because of its guilty association with man; now we bore the weight of its heavy sorrow — yesterday it had leapt in the wilderness, today it was tame and its hills and steppes had been stolen from it, at seven o'clock in the morning the lion, the desert hare, or the eagle that had been driven from the mountain could see Florence slipping by in her white silk clothes on her way to the golf course or the tennis courts; the lion watched mutely without even a murmur of complaint for man had taught him to submit in silence, but we bore the weight of his heavy sorrow — he knew it and Florence knew it as well; the tennis courts, the golf course were vast, vast, but neither the lion, the long-eared desert hare, nor the eagle approached them any more, having scented man from afar: there was a stench there, it meant death and yet seen from a distance it seemed — like

Florence and all the others — inoffensive, less barbarous at any rate than the eagle, the desert hare, or the lion who, hidden in grasses whose colours matched his own perfectly, stalked the choicest prey. But Florence was afraid now, we'll never be forgiven for that, she thought, never; they're all up there somewhere, all these beasts we've banned from our world are watching us, their conscience is clear and they are aware of all our crimes but in spite of everything they offer us an atrocious pity, a completely undeserved faithfulness, for the lion did his best to comprehend man's cowardice, he followed him along his path of destruction, trying to understand; yes, it was pity that incited him to climb into trucks alongside men, to become a tourist, it was pity but nobody realized it and Mike himself — Mike who was lucid, like all those who suffer in this world, all those whom pain convulses, moulds and constrains to its invisible, bruising yoke — not even Mike, thought Florence, knew about the particular form of pity nature offered him, who knows, maybe it was a sacred ignorance, and nevertheless she feared for him, for one day they'd come and rob him of that pity too, and it suddenly dawned on her that two curses that had besieged man all through human history were — when you gave it a bit of thought — incurable but simple disorders, the devastatingly simple evils called sickness and violence; at birth we inherit a violence composed of our very minds and breaths, she thought, our blood quenches its thirst day after day, while sickness is a kind of violence wrought upon us by a divine hand, which explains why it triggers our revolt: the only certainty that lies before the sick person is the stabbing certainty of his own death; the violent person can go on shouting and fighting it, but Mike no longer put up that kind of struggle, he had renounced the faculty of anger that belongs to those who are still alive; already gouged out as he was, purified by the light of another world, he let his dreams gather in his puny chest or, prisoner of the pain-racked cell his body had become, he dreamed for himself alone; as for Florence, she realized that her own malady was not fear of dying or of violence, but rather malignant memory working away at her, and didn't this beast that hid out in her heart thrive on vile images and servitudes? The innocent animals of the desert weren't the only ones who had carefully observed her gestures when she got up early in the morning, thinking to flee in the whiteness of her kingdom, all dressed in white against the red line of dawn as she went off to sully with her step the empty, chaste open spaces of the golf links and the tennis courts, feeling at home there; nature's innocent creatures, the lion, the eagle, had observed her for a long time, but they were in no way as formidable as the man, that companion of misfortune, who had accompanied her everywhere and who even now refused to die in her memories and in her heart; her former companion of pleasure now smothered her, with unfailing precision she had preserved every moment of his life, the complete legend of his past, his existence; having loved was just that, it was this merciless memory captive to every detail, and it didn't rush violently into your life but rather nestled into your soul with a slow, scandalous, obsessing fury; love and its pernicious fury, this weighty, useless dogma, was the only real evil in the world, thought Florence, and yes, she was afraid of that obscure thing love and its absurd slavery that had the power to threaten all beings — the soul, the mind, the breath, all died on contact with it. Objects, however, were less fragile than humans, they could be hurt but they managed to last, to outlive our difficult times; thus a pair of sandals in an empty closet came to Florence's mind, it was a distant, very distant recollection that nevertheless dazed her with the sudden awareness of the prophetic, often eternal role all objects play in our short-lived dramas; the sandals forgotten in a closet awoke from their sleep, those light objects suddenly assumed the heaviness of men and of vanished things, they began to weigh on her like feet trampling her body, and even if the sandals and the feet were only inanimate objects, dead things, still they had too much life in them, they shattered one's peace, violated the most personal physical intimacy, it shamed Florence but from now on she was alone with objects — the sandals, the feet she'd loved so tenderly — that had become ghosts, her ghosts; the sandals appeared in the closet and it was love once again, love coming back in another form, but the man was no longer there, he was far away, not even the dearest objects had detained him at home, his fickle feet now wandered somewhere else and the sandals that had for so long retained the imprint of a man, of a life, were love's final offering, the offering of a love which was no longer anything more than objects and derision; and that too forced you to abdicate, that too did you violence, no, I dreamed it, thought Florence, those tyrannical feet will not come walking towards me — whenever did I kiss, caress them? — but still there remained the luminous apparition of the sandals in the closet, the gush of tenderness for those gentle objects which would never learn evil in spite of the fact that we'd condemned them to share in our tortures; if Florence's memory dallied over that pair of sandals glowing in the darkness it was also because the image gave her a kind of repose, she'd known indulgence and rest near those tyrannical feet even if she now felt the need to deny the memory of that lost happiness — deny it because it was a vile happiness, it was desertion; gracefully bowing her head she had bestowed the gift of her lips, her pride and her soul on his ungrateful feet in a way that brought to mind those paintings and sculptures depicting so many proud souls prostrated at Jesus' feet, but those souls, thought Florence, hadn't been promised any of the happiness or pleasure she herself had known with a man; and Lucia went on scribbling in her notebook, Mike hardly saw her, he thought about the five police dogs in the yard, about Charlie who'd beaten him up one day and Gloria had said, "Forgive him, it's not his fault, he's just a brute," but a brute could also strike you, it was pure, unadulterated violence, it wandered, wandered everywhere, and Mike had tried to escape from the huge mass of cruelty that was bearing down on him, this nameless horror, Charlie, Charlie, and all of a sudden he'd found himself in his mother's embrace, she had hugged him, laughing, "There now, you see, there's nothing to be afraid of, get some sleep my angel..." and while Gloria clasped Mike in her powerful arms, he alone perhaps heard the tender words "my angel", spare, uncalculating words with no trace of maternal ostentation — for in this silence, this anguished wait, nobody knew that Gloria loved her son more than herself, that San Francisco and the motorcycle were all for his sake, and summer was coming, and she would be there to live all those dreams with Mike, those dreams that were of no use in the frozen space that spring's tardy rays teasingly lit up from time to time; they all said Mike was dying; if it was true — but no, he wasn't going to die since she loved him, he was her wealth, her happiness, no, he'd disappear only to come back again and he would always be Mike, she'd find a way to protect him, to keep him — but if it was true, why did they insist on crushing his dreams? When Gloria hugged her son, tenderly calling him "my angel", the delirious words, like the tiny roses that blossomed in the desert, were for him alone, and when Gloria pushed Charlie off, saying, "You'll rot in prison, you louse!" she was wicked, but she too was waiting for her deliverance, one of these dull days they'd come to get Charlie, take him off to a dull captivity, but that was all Charlie expected anyway: he hadn't turned twenty-five yet and the only thing he longed for was that descent into the abyss, he could hope for nothing more than a return to prison, escorted by two policemen and a dull record for he no longer even wanted to commit crimes, he begged silently, "Lock me up, keep me there, far away," but society didn't heed his wishes, they always let him out too soon, and Gloria took him in like all the others, they were dull human debris but they were still alive and breathing, she thought, who would feed them if she didn't, they came and gulped down her children's food, slept in her children's beds, mistreating them and beating them up as they'd beaten up Mike, and suddenly she was tired of it all, let them go back out into the street, she thought, back to prison, I don't care if the police come and take them away, lock them up, shoot them, hang them, but my son is mine and his dreams are my dreams, I gave him life, and Mike was somehow aware of her excessive compassion as it fell upon him, the huge body, arms raised towards the mute, insensitive sky, a woman alone battling all the demons of dread, and he fell asleep close to her, close to this heart blazing with a just and magnificent anger, fell asleep or at any rate took to breathing so lightly that she couldn't tell if he was living or unobtrusively slipping off into death. Maybe I'm not all alone in this underground, thought Florence all of a sudden, maybe he's looking for me, who's to say, maybe he'll come to get me here; there's Judith, too, who might find me here, she knows all about our nocturnal ways, but she was probably at the side of the burned young fugitive, he languished, languished, cried out in a bed of flames but you neither saw nor recognized the fire for his funeral chant was buried in the silence of the living and of the survivors, you could scream that way for a long time and nobody would hear you, for all men had to survive and all men were alone, even if most of them avoided suicide; I'm in a hostile world where nobody can understand me, Florence reflected, falling back into the shell of arrogance that defended her so poorly, she wasn't like these absinthe drinkers, like this lamentable flesh that prostituted itself day after day; she wasn't like Gloria, no, nor like the others, but she'd known that it all existed, she'd seen paintings, Degas and Lautrec were only painting life, they were glorifying flesh already threatened by death, these faces, she'd seen them only yesterday but now she understood why Lautrec had consented to his own internment, to detoxication in a clinic: he had become enamoured of the faces he painted, of that drifting pack, he had understood that they were to be loved and pitied; suddenly, through the exaltation of the transparent art of painting, by works that are seen and felt, all these things we prefer to forget—these faces, these destinies, these lives whose secrets and enigma the artist had tried to understand—came dangerously close to the visible world, to our indifference; and when art does violence to life in this way, when it goes to the very entrails of the earth in its search for itself, it's the creator, the artist, who must pay and suffer for that transparency—for Lautrec's prostitutes, like Degas' absinthe drinkers, were the transparent evocation of a race of men and women who would be submitted to our trials, those of our time, victims, like ourselves, of a social and individual apocalypse, and Florence thought yes, but now I'm meeting them all in real life, I could never have imagined that, we often forget, she thought, that we are the material the artist paints with, that he expresses us as we are and that the imaginary, or all that could be called invisible since we're blind to these things our eyes perceive every day, is everywhere, in misfortune, drought, cold or barrenness, and the imaginary is an obvious truth, we can't run away from it for our acts, even the hatred and scorn we feel for each other, reflect us all the time. It was noon and Berthe Agneli had to leave the campus to buy some books—cautiously, her eyes on the ground, she advanced towards the groups she had to pass, hoping they wouldn't see her, there were hordes of them, young people her own age who lived in broad daylight, in the radiant, perpetual sun, they weren't afraid, they lived in the open air and yet they hadn't lived at all she thought, she detested this springtime, its light and its abundance, all the signs of nature's feverish awakening that were associated with the blossoming of youth, nothing could be more painful than being young and overwhelmed by life when you didn't know what to do with it, when you found no better use for it than snuffing it out with petty, narrow ideals; they were there, passing close by her, it was early in the season, the spring sun was still new and they invaded the streets with their steps, their laughter, you could see them leaning over their bicycles, practically naked when the weather was still so cool, and she would have liked to tell them how much she abhorred them, them and their Grecian beauty, their wholesomeness, their self-assurance, how much she hated them all, boys and girls, those who were alone and those who were in each other's arms, the shifty ones and the solitary ones, none of them had ever been humiliated as she'd been humiliated, that's why they went to lie in the sun together, on the new grass, in this sun that just a few days before still slept in the winding-sheets of death, they disgusted her, they knew nothing of life, they hadn't understood anything yet; she felt a sad shiver running through her as she walked near them, and suddenly one of them called out to her, finding her pretty; she didn't know how to react to this kind of teasing, and their exuberance pained her for she had nothing to offer them, nothing to give, she had to preserve the little she possessed, it was so little and so secret, and they were irreverent, they couldn't understand anything; she thought of her professors, of the perfection they expected from her; was she not a kind of parasite with her miserably acquired scholarships, her mind already weighed down with knowledge she'd never put to use? — these other students lived in their own homes, in their natural surroundings, they had parents, friends, but she was alone in the world and without protection, she possessed nothing more than this hard, brilliant, arid mind that would very likely prove useless if she didn't graduate; she made her way carefully among them, thinking that her professors had probably noticed that she wasn't like the others — didn't they always answer her coldly, impatiently — only a few passed each year, maybe she'd be turned down, she and a few others, the chosen few of the Faculty Club went their way and she would go hers alone; on the other hand, perhaps her fears were unfounded, perhaps a nuclear sunset would expel all lives from the earth in a split second, yes, in just a split second; but in that case how could she justify the mistrust, the suffering, this Olympus-like university, when all these temples forbidden to the poor would be wiped out; what was the use of struggling, studying so late into the night while they went dancing in discotheques and had a good time, what was the use, she had nothing to give, nothing to offer, offering up the slightest bit of herself was a nightmare to her, even smiling, offering her hand, nothing, she couldn't, and could she possibly live any other way, and then, was it a dream or else an invention of her own hatred, but she thought she'd seen Lucia, Lucia who was thirteen, maybe a little younger, she hadn't seen them for such a long time, they'd always told her she was fearful, a hypocrite, her father used to speak to her that way, hypocrite, coward, he'd say, blowing the smoke of his vulgar cigar in her face, her mind had begun to live, like a pearl, a hard pearl, a sparkling, already dead mind it seemed to her, already dead to the joys of life, and the cigar smoke had stung her fine skin, suddenly Lucia, for it was Lucia after all although she hadn't noticed Berthe, Lucia had jumped into an orange Mercedes driven by a short, fat man whom Berthe could only see from the back; all that is over and done with now, Lucia, Berthe had thought, come back, but it was already too late, the orange Mercedes was carrying her off, who knows where, they were heading for the mountain still covered with snow, and Berthe had seen the slender form, Lucia, but suddenly they were gone, both the girl and the short fat man with his disgusting neck, the dark procession was already fading into the distance, Lucia, Lucia my little sister, and then that sterile light in Berthe Agneli's mind told her let them lose themselves, perish, you don't love them, indifference is our only salvation, she'd quickly forgotten Lucia, she had to buy all these books she didn't understand, work late into the night, law, studies, and they had disappeared in the direction of the mountain, into the mauve obscurity of the hills, perhaps they'd already left the city behind, Lucia, Lucia, and Berthe felt a presence nearby, a cat rubbing against her legs, he asked for nothing yet she pushed him off, it was too much, this package of shivering misery that had survived winter, the skinny limbs, the even skinnier flanks, it didn't ask for anything but it somehow exacted your pity, your attention, the cat moved off respectfully, his precarious lankness didn't get the better of him, his heart was pounding, he could barely control the frenetic movement of his jaw for all the birds were back in the trees, not all of them, but the crows and sparrows at least;

it took quite a bit of courage to come through all these harsh winters, he was a stray cat who had seen a few seasons and he wasn't about to cry or beg; the song of the birds made his heart beat softly, perhaps it was his last summer, melodious and gentle; stout, delicious birds, the taste of summer, would flock to the trees unknowingly, and he'd wait for them, his eyes burning with a great desire that nobody but himself would understand. So what if they were all heading for their own damnation, Berthe thought, Lucia and all the others, so what if they went on sinking calmly into corruption — the only way to get by in this life was to stick to the duties of cruelty and indifference towards others; Lucia was going to come to grief, but like the others Lucia would disappear in a puff of sacrificial smoke, she represented nothing more than a haphazard life, a graceful human form already consumed by vice; perhaps her own death was lurking close by, in the arms of that man who would snuff out her last hopes of innocence; Lucia was growing up, but she knew that everything around her was beyond measure: men, their desires, the superabundance of all these bodies she had touched and stroked, all the outrageous weight that had collapsed on her, silent or talkative, filled the excessive, intolerable space around her; Berthe Agneli stepped up her pace but the orphaned cat still followed her, it was above all reverence for her that moved him to follow her, for he scorned our small rewards, how could he catch all those sparrows in the trees with one sharp bite, his teeth couldn't trap them all at once but since they were all there why not let himself dream as his emaciated flanks sauntered easily along in the tepid day? God was good for He had created birds and squirrels; but as far as rats were concerned, it was a painful experience for a cat who longed for great things to stumble across those rigid, grey corpses that hadn't survived the throes of hunger, companions of a funereal winter who would never wake up to spring; and yet the rat, in spite of the hideous reputation with which we taxed him, was just as worthy of love as the cat; it was our fault if the rat had a bad reputation, he bore our shame and the stigmata of our long history, he had always been there at our side, sharing our wars and our hatreds, dying of our sicknesses, like us he had fought and resisted, he was a dignified animal and yet our servitudes had enslaved him, he had battered us and we had battered him; he was henceforth a part of ourselves, for in time and with the courage our degradation and misfortunes had inspired in him he had finally come to resemble us, and the discovery of a dead rat in a sewer sent a shiver of fear running through us for we recognized it as one of our thousands of cadavers, we felt in our bones that the rat's vile agony smelled of our secrets and our decay. During this time Florence was saying to herself maybe I'm wrong, I'm being hunted, death is hunting me, but I'm still in free terrain, yes, it's a mistake to cut myself off from everything that's human and withdraw from the side of the living; Mike, his mother, Tim — they all feel that I'm not with them, anything as inhuman as myself is an object of reprobation; Mike had turned his suffering face to her but he didn't seem to see her, he fixed his peaceful eyes on her without seeing her, his pupils slightly magnified in the light; even the tiny roses in the desert bloomed and survived and begged for air and light, just as Mike did

when he lifted his feverish forehead, his half-open lips
towards these gifts of life, but they didn't know it, who
could possibly comprehend the transparent, icy fervour
that had taken refuge in his chest, and they laughed, they
were gross, and Florence thought of those delirious
moments that catch us off guard between fever and
drowsiness and it seemed to her that she had found her
house again, in a dream, and each of the objects she had
loved was back in its place, even the painting with its
Mediterranean sky, it had all settled back into immobility;
a voice told her she could still go home, in peace, she could
still live and sleep there as in former times, could go back
to the absent words in the absent books that she liked to
spend whole nights reading, they were poisoned nights,
sleepless nights whose sole inhabitants were doubts and
mute, suppressed cries, but the books were vindictive and
formidable since to her they meant nothing but the dreary,
sonorous explosion of her own inner silence, of this
boundless, voiceless silence, this thing that went crashing
around deep down inside her, this thing she could no
longer name or describe that was her captive; even when
Judith Lange read to her patiently, the books spoke only of
things that were happening a long way off, far from her
terror, from her prison; she would even tolerate philosophy, there had been men and women in this world capable
of governing our minds when we couldn't even govern our
bodies, that was the role of superb arrogance, knowing
how to think, to exist, and Florence would say to Judith
Lange, all you've just read to me is true, they say it's the
truth, but that truth has nothing to do with me, maybe it
only applies to one man and not to others who are foreign

to him, but what a triumph when you are so unhappy, so downtrodden from birth on, to be able to construct a truth — it's discovering gold at long last under a mud-pile, but that gold is not made of flesh and blood, it's inter-mingled with the matter of the spirit and the spirit is frozen, and Judith Lange would say, but if men have written and believed certain truths for thousands of years perhaps they do exist, who knows, just as in spring a seemingly eternal lilac bush exists in the college yard. And Florence wondered what Mike was thinking about — he undoubtedly meditated too, like every living thing on earth; what could be going through his mind as he fixed his peaceful, absent eyes on her — his gaze was that of a vanished person and Florence strove to penetrate those unknown thoughts; that would be the first step back towards the side of the living, she thought, discovering the secret of the meditations and serenity shared by all those who were living in the shadow of death: it was something they all carried in them and they never spoke about it, perhaps it was just music nobody heard, but from time to time it floated right up to their eyes, to their faces, and Mike didn't dare move because he thought this scant happiness might escape; it was almost nothing: his mother, pausing in her unceasing agitation around the men at the bar, had smiled at him tenderly, and then her gruff existence had picked up as before, flexible and vigorous, she didn't represent men's thoughts, rather she was their well-spring and their pasture, she was their life, and yet, for a moment that had lasted no longer than a breath, she had stopped to smile at her son, and now life's bustle went on as before, as before, and Mike recalled all those nights when he lay tormented by a recurring nightmare while his brother Luigi snored heavily at his side—although there was a sovereign calm in Luigi's sleep that Mike envied and admired for it was the calm of nature, the calm of the sun coming out after a storm—it was always the same nightmare: Mike came home late at night like Lucia, he crawled along the barbed-wire fence of the yard to avoid waking the dogs but they leaped up at him, pretending at first to wash and lick him; there were piles of dirty snow in the yard and Mike trembled with fear for even if he begged the five wild dogs to stop their caresses, even if he said, look at me, I'm even wilder than you, don't touch me, you've scented the blood in me, don't come any closer, the dogs kept up their play, rolling over and over in the snow with him, and suddenly he was just a ball between their paws, he was hidden inside the sphere they played with but they didn't know it for they were only dogs, vigilant dogs, they had lodged him in the ball of snow and he could no longer escape, not even if he cried and screamed; and he woke up crying, and Luigi was still snoring.... Now that his mother had smiled at him so tenderly, however, the dogs had given up chasing him, the snow had melted, he was right there with his sisters, with all of them, maybe Judith Lange would come, she often came for a cup of coffee between two classes, and there was another being too, he wasn't ashamed of it, Gloria's smile had brought it back to his mind: it was a phantasmagoric creature but it had a human shape, it arrived just a few seconds before sleep at night, it meant shelter and welcome since it had arms, a face even if he couldn't make out the features clearly; above all it had a voice, since he heard it say, "Mike, little one, you can sleep now"; maybe it was mercy, mercy as we're unable to imagine it, roaming these cruel places where body and soul can no longer converse, having crushed and torn each other to shreds. Florence stared at Mike, thinking who knows, if Judith was right about the white lilacs, who knows, everything might be different, but she was no longer a child, an ascetic of reason, of a real world whose chains and limits she had always felt around her — the way one says, I usually go for a walk down that street, I've been living in this house for thirty years and in the morning I open my mail on the table — that heavy, dull reason was still present, even if the shock of desertion, of rupture had suddenly plunged her into this time of delirium with all these people; her reason in fact remained straight and proud, it was only her humiliated body that stooped towards the earth with them, and she thought, exercising her reason, I've left my house, my life behind me, I've broken out of my personal prison and I'm free, my only route from now to the end is wandering, waiting here, they don't know it, don't know that I'm in agony, Florence Gray the doctor's wife, that's all they knew of me yesterday; maybe he'll find me here, in that case we'd have to see our paintings and our furniture together again, even our son, we'd have to reconstruct the crumbling mountain of our lives — he was only a man, after all, no, he mustn't break into this silence that at long last brought her satisfaction, mustn't come while Mike, temporarily redeemed by his mother's smile, watched her so peacefully: he would arrive without warning, with all the noise and clamour of passion, with this right he'd had, that she'd also had with him, to make the other suffer, to say you

belong to me, your grave forehead, your mocking eyes,
you belong to me, he'd say it without saying it, and
suddenly she'd leave, she'd be his again, consenting to the
bewilderment of love, which is being unfaithful to all that
lives and breathes outside of the two of you, for living at
his side would be all that once again; he'd say you're tired,
you haven't slept for ages and ages; look, your son and I
were waiting for you, we are gathered around you, come
to us, come to me, he would be handsome and strong and
suddenly, while pretending to sleep at his side, to rest after
her long struggle, she would try to find a weak spot in him,
he had one, perhaps, his tanned hands on the white sheet,
how would they be joined the day of his death, what warm
perfume did they give off now, they were so perfectly
shaped but it was a weakness, he was mortal, he was
consuming himself rapidly at the altar of pleasure, the
pleasure he took with her or with other women, and
suddenly he was still, he no longer dared to move his large
body, he listened, watched, he too was fallible, passion's
executioner was dormant in him, but he was fallible; even
the rays of the African sun that bathed him as he made love
to Florence on a deserted beach, even that languorous sun
was already sprinkling ashes on his bones. But perhaps,
thought Florence, nostalgia was what ravaged so many
lives, even the nostalgia for what was fallible and mortal
around us since our sensuality in life was often just a
question of humble details, a smile, a gesture, these
infinitesimal gifts the earth offered to its passing guests,
and there was also the humble offering that was passed
from one person to another, from a man to a woman, it
had been such a small thing between Florence and her

husband, she thought, and yet it had been the emblem of her reason to live, of the stability of her heart, of her spirit, for a long time; and Berthe Agneli asked herself what was on the other side of the purple mountain and how Lucia could have the nerve, yes, the nerve to follow a stranger, to cuddle up against him, to take off with him like that, leaving no trace behind, or leaving nothing but an invisible wake of misfortune; she was no longer to be seen, there was no telling where she was hiding now, yet even this childish escapade must be part of some irrefutable order; perhaps Lucia's steps were being observed as they slipped off into the distance, her footsteps preserved in the silence of another world; you should always fear what you can't see, thought Berthe Agneli, and she was afraid of every-thing — of the bitterness, the anger she felt on this fine spring day when all of nature seemed in bloom; the joy of it somehow betrayed her, and soon it would be exam day, her judges would undoubtedly be as severe, as merciless as all the other judges she had known, how could you be good, how could men still dream of sainthood in such an absurd world; now she walked along without looking back, her head lowered, Lucia, Lucia, the cat also marched along the sidewalk, his nose lifted up to the trees, sniffing the fresh air that did him so much good — the trees were like a crown of hopes on his patient head, the birds so much hunger satisfied after such a long wait — and even if his hunger was satisfied in his mind alone it lightened his soul, he was suddenly seized by the drunkenness of spring; during the deathly December cold a woman had taken him into her garage, born poor, he'd nevertheless been blessed with this love, even though he was ugly someone had found him handsome, someone had spoken of his fine fur in spite of his thin, scabby coat; but spring fever had revived his wandering instincts long before spring actually arrived, and he had taken to the open air; and now, suddenly, his benefactress came to mind and he had regrets — well, other cats would come to replace him at her side during the deathly December cold, they'd come and sleep at her place during the long, slumberous winter, growing fat with contentment; like him they would wait for spring in the gentle paralysis of their tranquillity. And Mike thought of his walk in the park with Jojo, of the old tree he'd leaned against, of the spring fragrances that had called him back to life, he thought of the calm blue sky which one day, tomorrow or some other day, would stop changing forever; Jojo had been running in the park while Tim advanced tranquilly with his dog when suddenly the others had appeared: an extremely elegant mother and child who had probably come quite a distance for Mike had seen them emerge from the underground passage leading to the train station and make their way along the path between the trees, they didn't live in the underground passage, they emerged from it, golden and hazy in the sunlight; the child was about Jojo's age, three or four maybe, but he didn't resemble Jojo at all, he was dressed in a sailor-style coat and grey woollen shorts, even the buttons of his tiny coat shone in the sun, his mother held him by the hand but he squirmed every which way; the mother and the child, the sailor coat, the glittering buttons and the grey shorts that added dignity to the softness of his chubby knees were all pampered by the spring air — it was as though the trees had taken the two of them under their particular protection; Jojo watched them as if bewitched, sucking her grubby fingers, and Mike kept on repeating, no, don't touch that, don't put that in your mouth, no, and suddenly the little boy was there in his sailor coat, he was right there and his mother was close by, maybe she was aggressive, thought Mike, maybe she had problems even though she was a very young woman with a very young child; but only the child seemed gentle, although of course you couldn't tell how long he'd stay that way, he had thrown his arms around Jojo's neck with trusting delight: weren't grown-ups just distant peaks around them? — you couldn't embrace grown-ups the way he was embracing Jojo; the child had murmured to her, his words had the limpid ring of a savoury, foreign language even if it was the same French Mike spoke, the range of sounds that came flowing from the child's mouth was as transparent as crystal, my name is Stéphane, he murmured in her ear, Maman's name is Stéphane too, I don't go to nursery school yet; Jojo contemplated the exquisite, rosy creature in his sailor coat with its six buttons, she could count them by herself the way Mike had taught her, he said he was called Stéphane, like his mother, the trees, the sky, the pigeons, the whole earth was called Stéphane, Jojo listened to him mumbling the melody in her ear, such a handsome little boy who lived, like herself, on earth, and yet he was so unlike her, "Come, Stéphane," said his mother, "Papa is waiting for us at home, Stéphane, come here, obey me," and he pretended to listen to his mother, he went to her for a moment, kissed and cajoled her, and as soon as she let herself be distracted by these animated displays of emotion he ran back to Jojo, irresistibly attracted to her, to Jojo who smelled of the earth, grass, life; Mike was hardly watching her at all, he seemed to have fallen asleep on his feet, his hair blowing in the wind, yes, Stéphane, my name is Stéphane, and a host of pigeons swooped down near them, a solitary man had thought to feed them, the young woman with the aggressive look in her eyes was calling her son impatiently, but Stéphane and Jojo were running in a thick cloud of pigeons, they too were flying in the transport of their joy; Mike noticed that both the children's eyes had the same gleam, that their cheeks were the same healthy colour; the young mother suddenly relaxed a bit, she decided to sit on a bench and read while waiting for her son and from time to time, when the children approached her, she held out her hand as if to pick up her son by the belt of his coat, but it was only a game and he knew it, he just went on buzzing around her, me, my name is Stéphane, and so's yours, everybody is called Stéphane; from time to time the woman closed her book and looked at the child who so proudly called himself Stéphane, and her eyes clouded with worry again; he was right to refuse to go home to see his father, why did she still love that man, the child would soon be four, what would he be twenty years from now — an atomic blast and the child would no longer exist, tonight, tomorrow maybe, this marvellous being which had consumed so many hours, so many hopes, who was so malleable, so perfect, this marvel would be wiped out; it would be better always to see him as he was now, running through the pigeons' flight laughing and playing, having a good time like today, but who knew what perils, what dangers lay in wait for him, while he remained unsuspecting, how many happy years did he have left, would he have enough to eat tomorrow — if he reached adolescence would it be in a better world, or would he choose to drown his disappointment in us in alcohol and drugs? Laugh, have fun, you know nothing of all that yet, but she was cultivated and sensitive, she couldn't pretend not to know what kind of world this child whom she had created and so much desired was going to live in; perhaps he was already a victim of our century, already grieving beneath the luminous complexion, the tender lips, the rosy cheeks; the only child she saw was the one called Stéphane, in his sailor coat, the child she longed to dress like a prince, but for that she would need his father, at the very least she would have to see him once a year, on principle, to discuss Stéphane's education, the education of this child her eyes robed in gold and silk; Jojo she didn't even see, the sun darted its rays on Stéphane alone, Jojo was just an anonymous thing that liked to play in the mud, a forsaken thing, like her brother, miserable young wretches, she would no longer allow Stéphane to play with children who spoke so poorly, Stéphane would grow up to be a lawyer like his father, "Stéphane, darling, come along, Papa is expecting us, come now, my sweet," and he went to her, out of breath, murmuring in her ear my name is Stéphane and I don't go to nursery school yet, Jojo gave him a brief wave of the hand and he disappeared, Jojo's fingers seemed tiny and very pale in the light, it must be late already, thought Madame Langenais, even if daylight had been fading so slowly in the past few weeks, for Gilbert was finishing up his work in the garden, Madame Langenais could see the tip of his cap from the livingroom window; Gilbert usually didn't leave the garden when his work was done but lingered meditatively, for a long time, among his shrubs and flowers; and while this simple heart was preparing for summer, Madame Langenais enjoyed her solitude, oh, it wouldn't last long but this time, this space between the moment of her husband's departure and the return of her daughters, this time without voices or hubbub, contained just the silence of a gardener keeping watch over his own, for the creator of the coming summer wouldn't be God and His malicious rains or brutal hailstorms, no, the one who already carried the summer's crops in him was Gilbert, Gilbert and his knowledge of the soil, the friendly dust that he probed, caressed with his eyes, never growing weary of it, standing up against his hoe; and that silent time was an exultant bond, perhaps the sole bond, between Gilbert and the owner of the garden he tended, and Madame Langenais clasped her hands and thought maybe I'll have time to read a page of Tolstoy before the girls come home for supper, I even have time, why not, to listen to a Bach cantata, always the same one but I'm so slow, I started so late, Judith says, it was still daylight, the light no longer fell so quickly, it was all Judith's idea, a page of Tolstoy every day, the Bach cantata, every day an hour for herself, but did she have a right to that maternal egoism; reading Tolstoy became confused with Gilbert's rosebushes, with Judith, her steps in the house, her smile, Judith who had said, Maman let's invite Gilbert to lunch; she was no longer there, she could no longer talk to her, scold her while fixing her round eyes on her, it was always better to scold her since she had no respect for authority her father said, where did she live, not even her parents knew, it was such a beautiful cantata, she repeated the words without understanding them, *"Wo soll ich fliehen hin? Wo soll ich fliehen hin?"* It was a musical lamentation, a cry perhaps, but Bach's music, like Gilbert's silence in the garden and the future summer vegetation that lay dormant at his feet, this pagan music of the world — pagan even if a mystic had turned it into a sacred chant — seemed, to Madame Langenais, to be the very voice of her hope on earth, the voice of those glorious, epicurean and tranquil moments that proclaimed in the empty room, "Listen, listen for we are alive!" She would have liked to live this way all the time, in this interlude which admitted only joy, hugging Tolstoy's book to her breast, deeply moved, for it transported her, carried her back to an epoch that seemed to be hers — there had been a time when men had lived, fragile and stubborn at the same time, without making fun of the delicate nature of sentiments, but that epoch was finished, obsolete, they said — hadn't her own daughters told her so too, that that epoch was obsolete, and how could she defend them, protect them from the violent, outrageous things they saw and heard every day on the radio, on television, in the newspapers, from all that did violence to their candour, to their youthfulness, to their already wounded imagination, yes, did she herself not belong to another time, Josephine, Maman, I love you in spite of everything, Judith had said, why could she still hear her voice in this time and space that belonged to her alone, to her and to Gilbert out there among his flowers; didn't Judith's strength, and the vain combat they kept up in the girl's presence, come from the pressure of her fiery consciousness, because one felt scorched by the flame of consciousness she had maintained and cultivated, fanning it at first like a threatening spark smouldering silently in that secret soul; hadn't Judith always overwhelmed her with dogmatic questions, why am I here, where is God, why do thousands of my fellow beings die of hunger every day, what happened before I was born, why, why, and they didn't know how to respond to that terror that otherwise brought them so much joy; if only she hadn't learned to read so early, her father would have preferred to steer her towards medicine, it was a shame to have lost a daughter who understood everything but whose intuitive mind, unfortunately, all too frequently gave in to pride; and the flame had grown from a spark to a destructive, disproportionate fire, and Madame Langenais could no longer bear that blaze of consciousness near her — that's how, she thought, she had lost her daughter, she loved her deeply but she could no longer tolerate her presence; when Judith took her in her gigantic arms now, didn't she become just a capricious, scolding but capricious round-ness, just feminine charms made up of fears and offerings, yes, she was a bubble Judith longed to burst but why, when with her intuition Judith must sense the human matter she hoped to transform or unsettle was, like her mother, all of a heap and often defective in its behaviour, for nobody really mastered it, and in the end it always turned out to be the same vulnerable, transparent stuff? Madame Langenais expected Judith to be stubborn, for she knew that that stubbornness could become warmth and kindness if one knew how to seize its subtleness, she expected a bit of pity, of sympathy, otherwise she prefer-red that that streak of lightning go away and stop persecut-

ing her; she'd done her duty, she thought, by Gilbert as
well as by Judith, but Gilbert was leaning over his apple
trees in blossom, and Judith, rather than admiring the
architecture of the mediaeval cathedral she'd visited, as
her parents would have wished, recalled the blood that
had been shed on its steps, and it was as though the blood
shed by that rebellion, by the unsubjugated nation made
up of all the rebellious people of the earth, over whom
Madame Langenais had no power — she only saw them on
television or in the papers, and even from afar she was
afraid of them — it was as though this barbarous blood,
and it alone, could stir Judith to pity and sympathy —
sentiments of which her mother received only the austere,
ferocious gleam — and inspire her with a love that shattered her, for one couldn't love one's mother and condone
these massacres, not even in the name of justice, and yet
Madame Langenais knew nothing about her daughter's
ideas; more than once she had called her a Communist,
thinking that the accusation would send a shiver of alarm
and terror through the air, but Judith spoke very little of
herself and she had answered her mother with the mysterious smile Madame Langenais considered an insult, and
yet you're lucky, her mother said with dignity, when you
were only seventeen you had the chance to travel all the
way around the world — Josephine, Maman, don't be
angry, you know I love you — oh! keep quiet when your
mother is speaking to you, keep quiet and above all don't
laugh at me; Madame Langenais had opened Tolstoy's
book on her knees, but she had stopped reading already
and only Gilbert, in his garden, listened to the Bach
cantata; he didn't like music, the only thing he liked was

his rosebushes, but Madame Langenais shared that time of day with him, it was for him that she opened the livingroom window and said, "This moment is ours, Gilbert, listen..." and he listened, leaning on his hoe, all the while thinking about the birds, about the forest, thinking how the hunt endangered those he defended and loved—but with unwavering serenity, thought Madame Langenais, for it seemed to her that Gilbert, in joy as in chagrin, was always the same, not even his mood changed; all the rest of them changed, even her husband, and Gilbert was still leaning on his hoe, seemingly unaffected by the tumult, but why, she thought, yes why was her daughter so impetuous, she could have travelled like any other tourist but no, Madame Langenais should never have read the diaries Judith had kept of her travels, they weren't like anything, anybody, no, Madame Langenais had realized with horror—and she was still ashamed of her horror when it came to mind—that the only things Judith had retained of the history of the cities and countries she'd visited were tales of torture, the evil humanity had suffered in the course of centuries, just that and nothing more, she'd written it down, set it out in her notebooks with her icy, meticulous handwriting, maybe, her mother thought, in order to make sure she'd never forget to what fallen race she belonged, and the cry of her conscience was so strong, its radiance so cruel, that Madame Langenais still felt it throbbing close by her when she thought of her daughter's handwriting, when she thought of Judith's cajoling arms around her neck, that gesture she'd left behind like an echo of her deprived, trembling pity. But Judith Lange wouldn't come today, thought Mike, there had been his mother's smile, the rustle of all the others around him, shattering the cage of his bones; he hardly listened to them, hardly saw them, for all his immobile face contemplated was It, Pain, and he could no longer see them or share in their amusements or distractions, for the realm of life was fading away, crumbling, and yet from time to time someone passed — it might be Judith Lange, Gloria, sometimes it was a stranger — and shook Mike from his torpor, softly calling him out of his dim refuge: "*Allo, Mike, you are there?* Are you there, my angel? Are you hungry? Thirsty?" and he remembered once again that he was still with them, he was in a place built by men, in a house where people laughed and swore; a silent woman, sitting on the steps, looked at him without seeing him, for the monster of his pain had invaded the entire space of the house and he could no longer be recognized under the fetid mass of it; Gloria alone, perhaps, still knew him, for she approached him, patted his cheek, repeating the familiar sentence that pleased him — when you're handsome you don't feel like crying, you don't feel like sulking, you smile from morning to night; he knew that his mother sometimes drove off the fetid mass with that sentence, several times already she'd taken him away from the guardians of death that way, swooping down on him like an eagle in those condemned refuges, those hospitals for children with cancer, come on, why let them kill you with all that medicine, fresh air doesn't dare come in here because it's a poisoned garden, a garden in which they grow torment and breed torture; you're not going to perish here, my innocent flower...and, carried away in her arms, Gloria, the grasp of life itself, he fled towards warm, bright countries, muffled up in blankets; you won't be cold, there's a plane for Florida at five o'clock, and they flew over bare trees and a white desert, they soared over the walls that had held his pain captive, the pain that was his alone, they took off, the two of them, they'd never come back, it was so vast and bright down there, the birds sang, the perfumes of nature, rich and generous, wafted everywhere, you were showered with air and fruit, you slept with the window open, waking up at night to hear your heart beating calmly, evenly, and Gloria said, I promised you, didn't I, I stole you away from the guardians of death, just now they're leaning over your bed and you're not there, they can't come here, it's over the border, drink, eat, I'm not going to let you out of my sight, sure your head hurts a little, soon you won't feel anything, or almost nothing, the weight of my cool hands will make you forget the iron crown they tightened on your fore-head. Mike listened to Gloria's voice, maybe it was a voice addressing a deaf person but it was in communion with the desire he felt, with them all, against them all as well, to stay alive, to live out the opulence and the force of this desire to the very end, it was as if everything joined him in his desire, he was there beside her, with the air, the sky, the trees, the refreshing balm Gloria applied to his fore-head, and he felt the familiar leap of proud tenderness that won over all life forces; even old Tim, though he was now worn out by vice, had experienced the same thing in his native country, beside a woman, but it had happened such a long time ago that the red brick orphanage, the rock, the woman's embrace might now be just a pile of wreckage eaten away by the ocean — exile had dispossessed him of everything, even of his fellow-creature, a dog he hadn't been able to feed to the end; yes, when Gloria's voice brought the melody of the world, the song of the living, to Mike's deaf ear this desire to stay alive triumphed over everything, but there still remained the thing Gloria couldn't penetrate, for it was even deafer than her son's muted pain: when the body is submitted to so many trials it becomes a torture chamber, voices and cries beg in vain for entry at its threshold, for fright — hard, compact, and often relentless — is in ourselves alone; and so Mike had become deaf: he heard all these voices from outside but when he went back into that torture chamber he was alone with his executioner and had no way of knowing when or if, or for how long, the invisible presence would let him escape again, or even if he would ever find a time again — a few minutes, a few seconds — of gentleness such as he had felt before this season of torment closed in on him, taking hold of all the cells of his body; those cells had once lived their own lives, before they began to live off him all the while inflicting death upon him, and how could science hope to get rid of this executioner when each of these cells — these bodies haunted by ominous present-iments even during those moments in which the execu-tioner, harassed, took a momentary rest — when each was so distinctly separate from all the others that suffered from the same evil; when the chilled, tortured soul remained there in that separate room, cut off from all the other souls in this imprisoned body which didn't even have the soul's capacity to tell its own drama, its own story, for it didn't possess the language for that kind of narrative; when the body, thus shut up in a separate solitude, wandered around in search of a path, or sought its deliverance in annihilation? It often came at night, once Mike was in bed beside his brother Luigi, when Gloria was making love to Charlie or some other man, when the dogs finally quieted down in the yard after hearing Lucia's furtive footsteps fade away, then it was finally there, Mike no longer had to wait; and when the fever subsided and his mind cleared, he seemed to understand perfectly well just why an invisible dagger cut through his flesh: by his passage on earth, by this apparently unjust, senseless suffering, he had to obliterate all the crimes, cowardly or great, his father had committed; he'd had the misfortune to be born into this constellation of crime, and Luigi — sleeping now, and in sleep, when one no longer saw his eyes which carried all the seething violence inherited from his father, his profile took on an angelic air, his brown lashes like a shadow drawing out the eyelids, but it was only a diffuse, misleading image — Mike knew to what ends Luigi, the first Luigi's only true son, had been conceived, knew that the sinister story would go on without him; so that young Luigi could sleep peacefully, Mike was losing his blood silently, drop by drop, for the sake of the dead father and for the son who had inherited his instincts; for blood had been shed and more blood would be shed yet, and when it snowed or rained Mike imagined it was a torrent, a deluge of silent blood, the victims' blood refreshing the earth; he told himself that one day, sooner or later, in the spring, in the summer, the earth would finally be washed clean, and then he fell asleep, wondering if Lucia too could hear Gloria and Charlie groaning in the bedroom, it would have been better never to have separated himself from Lucia and Jojo, never; or did the blood his father had spilled — as a game, or out of daring, or just because it was the law of men among themselves — did this blood flow under the floors of the house, might they see it well up to the surface one day with its stench, its death-rattles, its sighs? Lucia wondered if Mike slept at night or if, like herself, he lay wide-eyed, staring at black spots on the wall; when cars went by on her side of the street her bed was flooded with light, she had the impression she was still participating in the movement of the street, the street that was her life, John's life, the life of all her friends; dawn meant hopes of taking off again with them, towards them, but she'd never see that man again, the man in the Mercedes, why didn't her nimble feet save her from all obstacles, "Come to my place with me, we'll see some dirty movies, little girls enjoy that,..." why hadn't she, so agile, learned to wriggle out of their grip, their brutal caresses? She'd been shut up with them before, a captive, but she'd understood that day, for the first time, that a man — and he wasn't even a vile man, he'd confided to her that he had a family — that a man and his strange virile power that she didn't under-stand had actually sequestered her, all the doors were shut tight, there were no chinks in their virile edifice, no way to escape, "Oh, come on, you're not going to jump from the sixteenth floor of the building, the windows don't even open because of the air conditioning, but why are you afraid of me?" and yet he was just a fat man, in no way wicked, he was divorced and lonely, the thought of taking Lucia home with him had comforted him, his fleshy neck didn't please her, he was an odourless man who lived in an odourless place, he had hardly approached her when, for the first time, terror seized her, why hadn't Gloria ever told her about this feeling that shook all your defences, she invoked Gloria in vain, her bound fists and soul battering invincible surfaces, isolation, a man's caprice, Gloria wouldn't come to the rescue; later, running along the streets without knowing where she was headed, with the terror still in her, throbbing in her chest, she'd lost her courage or rather the audacity that up till then had depended on her ignorance because she realized how abandoned she would be from now on, on this earth, abandoned even by Gloria, and as for the money for John's acid, from what humiliated sweat was it wrung, she had collapsed in a restaurant where a woman had had pity on her, my name is Gabrielle Dubois, I'm a waitress, you look like you're afraid of something, I'm about to close, I've been on the job since six this morning, don't worry about the coffee, I've got a few clients who can't pay, here, have a glass of milk as well, but a woman can be a waitress without losing her dignity, you know; I used to be a schoolteacher in my village, the village was wiped out, they built those dams there, and we haven't been able to see the sky since, I started another life here; the melody of the street came and went, in rain or snow the cars went by, lighting up the silent wall Lucia stared at with feverish eyes while waiting for morning; Jojo was right there and yet she might have been in another world, in a galaxy of sleep from which she would never return — hadn't her tiny shape been encrusted in the pile of clothes and toys Gloria had thrown pell-mell into the depths of night? and the tiny shape that the night illuminated from time to time was no longer Jojo, Jojo provoking the flight of the pigeons in the park, her whole, delicate life inebriated with the dizzying density of things she'd felt during the few minutes spent with the magical Stéphane, no, this was the little Jocelyne as her sister had always known her, fallen into the depths of night with her few mutilated toys and clothes, capsized, here or in another world, in that strange galaxy, perhaps nothing more than a shivering form bound to her sister by their slight, similar breathing and their thick hair intertwined on the pillow like an offering; out on the street the melody came and went, light and passers-by in constant motion, it was a tremendous noise, and Jojo's delicate breath hovered in space without reaching her for you left life when you slept, and Lucia finally dropped off to sleep, Gabrielle Dubois, the waitress at the *Steak House*, would be getting up shortly, she got up at six o'clock every morning, she saw I was afraid, that my hand was shaking, the coffee was scalding, watch out, don't spill it all over the place, here, let me help you drink it, at last Lucia closed her eyes, at last, an act of pity, she had been given that at least; but Gabrielle Dubois was an honest woman, Lucia would never be able to tell her about John and the others; she slipped off, joined her sister in a serene, childlike sleep, and Mike thought that Charlie — even if Mike didn't like him, even if his nature was a kind of dough in which all villainies would impress themselves one day — in spite of the yawning cowardice of his personality, was also innocent in his fashion, like a ravaging beast dragging his wounds after him; was it the whip, or misery, that had made him stoop from birth? If he no longer felt the desire to make love it was because he'd learned to die young, Gloria said, and every time she obtained his release from prison he wanted to return as soon as possible, for the word liberty pounced on him like a vulture, all that terrorizing space had to be filled, what would become of him beneath the vast sky he had always contemplated through bars, shouldn't he crawl like an insect, seek even greater humiliations, and Gloria said eat, act like a man, try to straighten yourself up, but he shuffled along, stooping ever lower, with envious thoughts for those who would be executed in his stead by gas or hanging; he wasn't afraid of those blood-red dawns, for they meant you left the cell behind, the cell that was nothing but waiting and livid fright, this waiting when you had a craving to loot and kill but lacked the courage to do so, you waited and waited, obtaining nothing more than a few pitiful whiffs of triumph in the course of token crimes, and the handcuffs they slipped on your wrists, which quelled for a time the burning desire to kill. Charlie often got up at night and went downstairs, Mike could hear his prowling footsteps in the kitchen; what went through his mind in the bitterness of those winter nights, what was he thinking of, prowling, prowling cautiously under Gloria's roof, Lucia was sleeping close by, maybe he was thinking about Lucia, maybe Charlie had regrets, for there were very few executions during that sterile season in which the earth took on the whiteness of lilies; judges were so cruel, he thought, that in America and elsewhere they preferred to elect their candidates for the guillotine or the electric chair in the spring or summer when they themselves were about to take their vacations, for shortly after prescribing the final solution — the only solution that had seemed reasonable and useful — for his patient, the judge suddenly felt the shiver of the death-agony he himself had engineered from the invisible ramparts of justice; the man he had thought to deliver from himself remained an invisible pariah but all of a sudden the judge felt himself pursued by invisible blood, the colour of which he had never seen much less sniffed the odour, a host of invisible maledictions plagued him and he had to get away, flee, quickly, no matter where; the judge and his wife hurried away from their domain besieged by angry appeals, taking off so suddenly that the children were left behind with the servants, domestics who had come from the most leprous corners of the earth to serve them and who asked for almost nothing for they too were invisible pariahs; the judge and his wife were known in the district for their generosity and their clemency; the woman was an alcoholic and given to crying in secret, the man was still young and ambitious and didn't cry, but his invisible burden haunted him, however harsh, cruel, and upright he might be, and even when he went off to some secluded island with his wife, who would go on drinking and crying in secret, even in his island paradise he would have the feeling he was being implacably watched and lacerated by the invisible pack he'd nurtured and maintained, for in purging the universe of its assassins, did he not at the same time dispense an unexpected manna, did he not provide an indispensable, hygienic purification in this desert where men's moral qualities no longer blossomed? As far as men being good or bad went, the judge hadn't created them and had no responsibility, he did no more than make the decision to exterminate them when it was deemed necessary, he had nothing to do with the creation of men, he was only a judge, a purifier, he would like to fumigate the earth and rid it of man completely; it seemed to him that the world could become a place inhabited by omnipresent order and justice, he imagined himself alone, the way he'd hoped to find himself on his island, with no children, separated from his alcoholic wife — for his wife with her silent crying, her tragic face, carried with her everywhere the phantom of that "adequate conscience" of the men he scorned — he imagined himself alone with nature, and the only thing that saddened him when he thought about the men he'd condemned waiting in their cells was the haunting wonder of the spring or summer they wouldn't live to see; day after day his secretary brought him letters bathed in supplications and tears but he never read them: he won't see summer, your honour, can you imagine what that means to my son, he's not even thirty yet — wretch, leave me alone, he thought, pushing the letters away with a wave of the hand, he had to get away immediately then it would all happen a long way away; perhaps the judge and his wife had even forgotten it, for they were resting, the phone was no longer ringing day and night, his secretary had stopped sending him letters and the children, who weren't old enough to understand, were basking in the warm California sun; no enemy, no prowler would come to harass the judge and his wife beneath their bedroom window, no, it had slipped out of their minds, for nature's order erased everything, what gardens, what splendour, they exclaimed in low voices; they'd forgotten and in the meantime it was winter and the nights were long, and Charlie prowled in the kitchen, the judge had forgotten this nasty, snickering prowler now left to his own solitude;

Charlie opened the paper, usurped as it were the criminal who had been condemned to the electric chair, "When I think that little Michel Agneli, with his tumour, will kick the bucket slower than this guy!" would it be this week or later — later, thought Charlie, on one of those nice spring days, one of those mornings when everything springs back to life, a sparkling dawn, not everyone had a right to the celebrations of spring and summer, what would the judge have decided if he'd known the well-mannered, bourgeois boy who'd been in Charlie's cell-block in the penitentiary just a few months before, of whom Gloria had said, "That's no bum of your race, no good-for-nothing, oh no, he's a real prince who stumbled in there by accident," this prince with the satin skin and musician's hands, who'd raped a five-year-old girl in the woods, very respectable, yes, and Charlie smiled, scornfully squashing out his cigarette, the prince's mother and sisters were gentle and refined, they came to visit him every Sunday; when you saw Charlie, Gloria said, you could understand why he'd spent his life in prison, but in the other case, no, it seemed incomprehensible, crime was his taboo, his mystery, Gloria would have taken him under her wing but his was a proud nature that couldn't be tamed or conquered; all life offered her were shameful messes like Charlie — and yet it was the link between colourless Charlie and his colourless crimes and the mysterious criminal surrounded by friends and relatives that permitted Gloria to cross, for the first time, the social boundaries that had always kept her at a distance from the joys of privilege; suddenly, thanks to Charlie, she found herself in the company of the powerful, and in the whirlwind of hatreds and disputes her life was made of, it suddenly seemed to her that during that halt she'd felt something like love. It was so nice out, what time could it be, wondered Monsieur Langenais as he headed for home on foot, for with the arrival of spring he'd taken to walking home from the clinic, and Josephine appreciated his discernment and absence for she had had the impression that the family — with the obvious exception of Judith whom she hardly expected any more, and only on the occasional Friday at that — rushed home to burst in upon the radiant silence of her late afternoons, when she had Tolstoy to read, Bach to listen to, when she needed time, and she had wondered why Charles so rarely used his legs when he'd been so athletic as a student; and suddenly he was walking, attentive to the rhythm of his stride, not as tired or worried as he would have expected, a successful operation made for a good day, he'd tell Judith that, she'd probably make fun of him but her complacent, silent smile pleased him, why insist on changing young people, maybe they were the only ones who really made sense, his wife should have suggested these invigorating daily walks sooner — until now he'd been unaware of the charms of his city, of his neighbourhood, when you left in the car in the morning to drive the girls to their private schools you didn't see anything, why the luxury of private schools, it was another of his wife's ideas, a maid, a gardener, private schools, why private schools when his daughters were so lazy, he went slowly up the fragrant avenue lined with bluish lilacs in full bloom; how strange it was to see those foreign words posted in the hospital corridors, "Pain Center", the English words struck him all of a sudden, "Pain Center", "Pain Center", and yet nothing could be more true, and at the same time, stopping to contemplate a dazzling patch of red tulips at his feet, he thought, we were so slow to understand the art of enjoying life, or was it Judith's voice he heard? — in times past they would talk late into the night, Madame Langenais had even been jealous of their conversations, to such an extent that she had read, in secret, all the philosophers the father and daughter quoted to each other; Judith had been so eager for knowledge that they had had to add shelves to the livingroom library; I have no idea what will become of her, thought her father, where our own children are concerned such things escape us; he was extremely fond of Judith but he also had fearful doubts that kept him awake at nights, misgivings he never mentioned to anyone, he was afraid that they'd given birth to an exceptional being who might justify their worst fears; perhaps he thought once again of the patients he'd operated on that morning, as Judith had taught him, maybe he was overly affected by the word "conscience" that she was always using; unlike Judith, he was no longer at the peak of his life, she seemed to forget that he was already on the decline, he thought, he could no longer keep up with his children in athletic competitions, and it suddenly struck him as odd that he should devote so much time to other people's troubles and the scrupulous study of their weak points when he knew so very little about himself; the evanescent patch of tulips had fixed itself now in his mind, from that moment on it would be nothing but an image, the fleeting image of this fine spring day, and while the memory of the flowers rooted itself in his mind Monsieur Langenais listened to his own heartbeat; he seemed a frail man but his appearance was deceiving for he was strong, sometimes he still thought that his vocation as a healer had marked him with the sign of immortality — physical immortality that is, for he didn't believe in any other kind; his wife in no way shared his theory of nothingness after death but it would have been useless to contradict her in her religious candour for she was a woman of another world after all — and breathing in deeply, he continued along the bright, sweet-smelling avenue, immortal, yes, that was it, like today and nothing more, it was Judith who had spoken to him of the elevation of thought, of Kierkegaard's mind soaring to austere summits, she never invited her parents to her place, they didn't even know where she lived, birds were chirping, children shrieking joyously in the streets, why hadn't he taken notice of all this activity sooner; it was true that in winter he never recommended such rigorous walks to his patients, he was responsible, weren't they entrusting their hearts — its pulsations, its worries, its turbulence — and his too to the dexterity of his science, all in the hope of improving their survival, and their survival on earth, as Monsieur Langenais saw it, meant a fleecy eternity of small but concrete joys; and now he experienced gratification on this ordinary day lightened by modest joys, he felt it when he thought of Judith, when he thought of his wife who had told him to wear his grey striped suit that morning: he had to be told everything, like a child, she had mumbled, and then, he recalled, he had forgotten himself for a moment, he had scolded Marianne who was feeding the poodle with cookies she was dunking in her hot chocolate, he could still smell the fragrant, steaming chocolate; and why, when he listened to his own heart, this principal, transparent organ, why was he so faintly aware of its mystery as he listened to it live and dilate in the tunnel of his own body, when he knew it so well in others and was so familiar with all the exhaustion and vexations it could survive? He thought too of his son but with less certain pleasure for he didn't really know him very well, he was in France, another of his wife's ideas, studying to become a sociologist — if he had been born in another country the same son might have known a harsher fate, his life might have been governed by the laws of war, subjugated to a scornful, virile authority that would have transformed his nature, and under a flaming sky the same boy might have learned to kill very young, like so many others whose hopes had been sacrificed for their elders' profit — no, Monsieur Langenais' son was no barbarian but his father couldn't say just who or what he was either; and the whole time, time that flowed on across Mike's profile as the boy stared unseeingly at Florence still sitting on the stairs, for he was set before her, it seemed to her, like a statue, like some manifestation of a blind, spiritual world, although a real face, still alive and expressive, transparent in its set emotion, shimmered in the air and by moments seemed to become attainable and Florence's hand reached out towards it but she couldn't draw anything human close to her inert, passive limbs, and they can't help seeing that I can no longer feel anything, she told herself, all this is fine, going off, deserting, and the whole time, she thought, that man believed I belonged to him but it was a lie, even if he came back now I wouldn't budge, wouldn't forsake my stiffness, my decency, no, I wouldn't leave these stairs at all, he'd say to me, here I am, don't you remember me, and I wouldn't answer, he must never come back, he was all the crazy, excessive tumult of passion, the isolated fever that could separate or kill two people, time had come to a stop around Mike and her, there was nothing threatening here; Mike, Gloria, old Tim, Lucia, they thought of her, they brought her food and drink, but she was no longer hungry or thirsty, only ashamed, she was no longer captive of a man, of love, but still she didn't know how to extricate herself from life, how to fling herself out of life in one brief, final jolt without offending those around her; they would understand her decision here, it was a haven of compassion for captive or desperate people like herself, Lucia was saying to her mother, "Look, the sun is all red, you'd think it was summer already"; and Tim, who was still crying, blew his nose with a thunderous noise and said, "He'll never come back, never"; "Come on, Tim, *old boy,*" Gloria said, "*it was just a dog,* even if he had more dignity than his master, that's for sure..." but Tim had dashed outside, shouting there he is, it's Tim; it was a dog like him, or maybe just a dog who had emerged from the vapours of Tim's alcoholic consolation, and old Tim, his pornographic magazines under his arm, followed Tim the dog, one of his own kind, they had the same weary pace, the same shaggy coat, "*Old boy, old boy,* come when I call you, it's me, Tim...." Tim called him again but in vain, either the dog was too exhausted to respond or else Tim had dreamed it, and old Tim just missed being run over by a horse and carriage but he continued to pursue his vision, a blissful smile on his face; the horse drawing the carriage was bitter and thin and just as old as Tim—dragging his broken, winded carcass in the dust, giving the impression that nothing could weigh more than the load of tourists behind his flanks — it would have pleased him to kick old Tim to the ground but he turned his dark, oblique glance away from him, let him cross and then continued along imperturbably beside the sidewalk, passing the park, the Hôtel des Voyageurs, for how much longer yet, he wondered and he plodded along, slowing his pace, summer was such a difficult season with the dust that dried everything up, with thirst and flies, those black clouds that mingled with your saliva, no, Jojo, the pebbles aren't for him, he's a horse, you understand, those children with their games, their piercing cries, couldn't ever understand that he was an old horse, they had no respect for the dignity of his species, old Tim berated him impudently, "*Old bastard, old bastard,* hey, watch where you're going!" — it was the very vertigo of the street that pleased Lucia so much, the summer dust, the dirt and flies, it's like summer, she had told her mother, everything is red, but Gloria hadn't had time to look, "Come help me wash the glasses, Lucia, I've enough trouble what with your sister at the university, the snob, making up poetry, for crying out loud, with all the junk they stuff into their minds in that place nowadays!" and Florence, who could see that Lucia was disappointed, heard the words vibrating deep inside herself, they were part of the conspiracy of stupidity and brutality that marred our lives, she wasn't thinking of Gloria — her stupid, brutal words were something foreign, like Mike's expression against the window at the other end of the room even if his ethereal, ascetic look was the very opposite of Gloria's words — but one might have said that

that stupidity, that brutality was sinking deeper into her,
that she was suddenly aware of how easily you could
crush, maybe even permanently, the delicate impulse of
hope, and she felt tremendously exhausted, for herself as
well as for Lucia who felt so let down; Florence closed her
eyes, once again saw her room, the book she had left open
on the night table, the untouched pack of cigarettes; what
would become of all the objects that were waiting there, of
the painting with the Mediterranean sky, perhaps her
entire past, perhaps her life was just a trembling image that
would fade away with time like the tones of the painting
she had liked; furthermore, as her look clouded over, the
room lost its clearness, became less well defined in her
mind as if a whirlwind had dissolved, liquefied something
which only the day before, when she had still been there
among her things, her possessions, had still had form, a
silent geometry that haunted the desert of her life. How
abandoned those objects, all those things her hands and
eyes had caressed and kneaded day after day, must feel
now, thought Florence: an undisturbed bed, a lamp keeping watch over no one, and the books, the faithful books
would be forgotten now, nobody would open them to
dispel the anguish of the night; but what was happening to
the others during this time, what had become of the girl
who'd been cold all winter, the frozen creature Florence
had seen sitting on a yellow bench in the middle of the city
with her heavy suitcase at her feet, who had smiled at her,
that filthy girl smelling of wine, was she still alive — yes,
undoubtedly, she and the man with the cane as well, the
man who seemed to loom up out of some wintry, nocturnal path to advance so painfully in the afflicting daylight;

now that spring was coming, maybe he'd go and sit on the yellow bench, staring at the sky discontentedly, for you never perceived the end of your troubles on the horizon, not even when you'd lived almost a century; life was no bait for a shrivelled-up old man clinging to his cane, no, it could attract only the frivolous young creatures who were fluttering around him, running in the grass, playing ball, having fun, it was all so noisy, so odious — maybe the drunken girl who'd been cold all winter was doleful and gentle when she came to sit on the yellow bench; Florence thought of them all, it was Tim, slamming the door in the coolness of the day, who had evoked all the whisperings of the street for her, Tim who was heading for the racing, feverish life outside in search of his lost dog, jumping about in his drunken enthusiasm, and just as he had seen his dog's double, he saw, a few seconds after passing a vagabond all dressed in black, another vagabond who, although he must have been twenty years older than the first, resembled him like a brother; Tim vaguely recalled vagrants who lived in the subway all winter, maybe these were the same ones he'd seen there, and now they were like dark subterranean animals coming up towards daylight; Tim saw their muddy silhouettes all over the place and they seemed a threat to him, these drifting ghosts reminded him — as Tim the dog had reminded him — that winter would arrive once again, reminded him that he in turn might become one of these reeking, filthy, underground scarecrows, and maybe they had recognized him, for they greeted him in passing; the younger vagabond, the first who had emerged from the night, had appeared to Tim like a sacrilegious incarnation of his own downfall, or

the downfall of the city that had become one with himself,
he was the underworld in the sun, Tim thought as he saw
him again, leaning against the wall of a department store in
black ragged splendour, his eyes still clear and malicious,
his teeth sharp, standing there with a battered black hat on
his head, his black, curly hair that neither comb nor water
had penetrated in months now seeming to invite the
light's caress; he held a bunch of yellow flowers like an
offering in his blackened, open hands, as if, thought Tim,
this dark subterranean ghost had a right to hold flowers.
"Shit the young bastard," he snarled, hiding his face to avoid
seeing him. The second vagrant Tim saw was as dark as the
first, all dressed in black like his predecessor, but he bore
no sign of interior brightness; like the first he was a
rag-man walking joylessly, heavy and alone towards the
summer light; Tim told himself that it was his own weak
soul coming towards him and he averted his gaze though
he hadn't always looked down upon those he angrily called
"flea-ridden rag-bags"; a host of beggars and drunken
poets still ran through his imagination, it was back in the
time of his idyllic childhood, they were men, his fellow
countrymen and they invited him to drink with them...it
was a drunken, fully-clothed orphan diving into the sea,
the Ireland that was so far away, it was a throbbing echo,
the voice of a brother, of a friend, the sound of the waves
at night...exiled, exiled and where would he sleep
tonight, maybe in the park but his dog wouldn't be there,
maybe at the Hôtel des Voyageurs if Gloria took pity on
him, but she didn't always take pity on him, it was true
what she told Lucia while she washed the glasses, "With a
bit of luck, a girl can make around $25,000 as a topless, you

listen to your mother's advice, of course you gotta give a good slice of it to the boss. . . ." "Yes, it's true, Maman," said Lucia, but she was barely listening to her mother, Florence observed, she came and sat at Mike's feet and sighed, "Think I'll go out for a walk." "Where?" asked Mike, but she was already in the street with her boots, the frayed hem of her jeans, she was leaving, he could no longer hold her, and Florence felt Mike's tormented look upon her, imploring Lucia in silence, where was she going? "*Peace and love,* that's all I want," John told Lucia and he seemed relaxed as they drank their milkshakes in a student café where they both felt sheltered, "We went to the Carabinier, I bought some white dust there, sniffed two lines in the men's room. . . . I don't remember what came afterwards. . . . Then four policemen were waiting for me outside, they took me to Saint Justine's Hospital. . . ." Lucia listened, listened to this enigmatic language that had become hers; lately John's escapades frightened her, topless, $25,000 a year, but you didn't make so much if you were scared, her mother had told her so, but then there was also Gabrielle Dubois who'd told her in the *Steak House* that if Lucia was ever in danger she would be glad to take her in; but the fear, who could understand fear, she'd always be afraid, she was no longer under Gloria's protection and the future was nothing but fear, all encompassing, *"That's life,"* John was saying, and Lucia thought of her sister Berthe, where was she, at what university, how could she find her, but John was lighting a cigarette, still talking about the white dust, you forget everything, he said, and it was as if the sound of his voice was gradually thinning out, like himself, Lucia listened to him with fright

— escape, disappear, *"peace and love"* — yes, but wasn't this transparent oblivion he pointed a finger at a secret path to horror? I'm deaf to everything, thought Berthe Agneli, stepping up her pace for the ungainly cat was still prowling from one tree to the next making believe he wasn't following her, an expert at this game of nonchalant dodging, stopping from time to time and carefully licking his coat under an oak tree, at such moments appearing exclusively preoccupied with his feline well-being and completely indifferent to man's world; at other times he drew his claws and lunged at the tree trunks in a rush of defiant guile like a giant beast but he wasn't a giant beast any longer and he fell back into the grass with a plop and set to licking his paws, purring, and then took up his serene pace once again; Berthe Agneli felt his sneaking, watchful presence close by but she repeated deaf, deaf, yes, what do I care about Lucia and the others, Michel wouldn't suffer so much if they gave him some liquid morphine every day, it's permitted for terminal patients, but maybe they've just forgotten, she thought, and she, like a walker whose footsteps fade away in the sand, was a long way from all of them now, far removed from their corruption, she was studying in one of the city's English universities where they'd never find her, they didn't know that she was living in foreign territory just a few blocks from their home; she could barely understand what she studied at night, but did understanding really matter, wasn't success her only goal? Only a few passed each year, she lived in an anonymous city whose essence seemed to be of mineral rather than human origin, she had no friends, her only hope was a cold, inorganic success, she would only see her professors on judgement day, they would ask her questions without looking at her, they got together at lunch and also around five o'clock in the evening sometimes, no student was permitted to share their evening intimacy, at least that's how Berthe perceived her intellectual surroundings; sometimes it seemed to her that there were a great many of these mineral weights on earth, they were human in appearance only: every morning each of them opened cold blue eyes and turned them towards you, spoke in embalmed, prepackaged sentences, and it took a long time to realize that their seemingly non-aggressive hands, words, teeth, and hair, that those lips always prompt to pronounce analytical, disarming definitions, were inorganic, mineral, nothing more; and if you were of humble origin, Berthe thought, the only way to avoid falling victim to their icy, systematic destruction, which could be accomplished with a simple word or look, was to assume their own cold, absent attitudes — didn't they require that you too carry out that amputation of self that affected them so little? After exams, if she graduated, Berthe Agneli would in turn become a member of this mineral world, and would therefore be free and intact for life, the competition and the victory would be forgotten, each of us has his silent death in life, but above all she would never again let anybody offend or touch her, she would be deaf to all their lamentations — but if only they gave Mike a little morphine every night he'd be able to forget — the important thing was to attenuate every flick of consciousness, for reality wasn't sensitive, we were the ones who were too sensitive to it, Berthe thought, the cat was still silently sniffing out adventures in the grass, he knew the city's secrets better than anyone but he rarely came to stroll near the campus in spite of its comfort, he preferred the underside of the city, the shadow of its bridges and cellars; after leaving her village Gabrielle Dubois had found herself a lair near the Jacques-Cartier Bridge, you could live there on practically nothing, she said, and from her window you could see the gigantic bridge, its pollution, and the river down below, but as for the only *real* river, maybe she'd never see it again, that's the way she'd spoken to Lucia, I've got a lair under the Jacques-Cartier Bridge and it's a good thing cats come hunting the mice and rats in the summer; the cat was quite familiar with that zone of desires and poverty, he'd been seen roaming around there with his brothers, neither handsome nor ugly but a ferocious fighter, and yet he wouldn't go back under the bridges for wasn't the glory of wild cats to be found in conquering the walls of the big cities, braving all their perilous crossings and distances in princely fashion and then slipping unnoticed through the trampling human crowds? Some of them perished that way, crossing a bridge, a highway, a wall, in those pitiless steel and iron hunting-grounds; for this race of fragile creatures — soon distracted by the din and call of the open spaces, separated as they were from their woods, from all the warm retreats which had protected their nerves for so long, from the foliage whose colour matched their coats — it was the insidious call of the wild open spaces that drove them to the bridge that stretched out over such an interminable distance, and to the highway, and from the soaring bridge, from the dusty strip of sand at the edge of the highway, a simple cat could

see the river and the sky, the entire rose and green city
emerging from its misty basin at dawn, and the cat would
go on with a troubled heart, eager for ecstasy and forgetting that death was speeding towards it, so terrible that
when its body exploded under the wheels that shattered
it, it merged with the road, with the sky of liberty that it
had adored a moment before, and the spray of bloody
fragments staining the road would never blossom, no
dream would arise from it, for it was thus that men killed
and killed, with this blind, deaf rhythm, they and their
gestures engulfed in the repetition of their crimes. Maybe
it's true, thought Florence, maybe one experiences more
in the hours or minutes of a fulminating death-agony than
during one's whole life, I hope I won't bungle it, if it's a
rope around the neck or a bullet through the brain, get it
right, the exact spot, yes, my husband would put his hand
on my heart saying, right there, only there, not anywhere
else; Mike had left his chair to help his mother in the
kitchen and the chair remained there in the red space, an
unsociable thing, yet it had learned to live among people
and their ways for Florence thought she heard it creaking
silently though neither Mike, Jojo, nor Lucia was there to
lean against it or make it bend to their capricious limbs; if I
make you some meat juice, Mike, will you drink it with a
straw, it's for your own good, you know, Gloria was
saying, and all these murmurings came and went around
the empty chair in the kitchen that would seem emptier
still when Mike was no longer there at all, Mike with his
frail legs, his body like a stunted plant, and the face he
turned towards the luminous window all day long; Florence wondered if Mike, like painters and writers who are

often born with a knowledge of humanity's tragedies long before they actually come to pass, had perhaps had a premonition of the drama he was going to live — always a witness, always suffering — a long time ago, when he was still in Gloria's womb, but she, Florence, had never had the slightest conscious or unconscious presentiment of her future unhappiness, had been touched by no forebodings, and now she reproached herself for that lack, for her misfortune, so sudden, so rash, seemed all the greater for it — you could never rid yourself of it, because it had taken you by surprise; and yet she had intuitively been aware of the presentiments of others, presentiments that certain precocious or timeless consciousnesses — they didn't fit into the realm of common vision and Florence was unable to define them — had expressed through art or writing: Kafka had revealed to the world the underground layers of this earth on which we thought we could dance at our ease; writing was an underhanded weapon, it came to denounce furtively, digging its mute dagger into the inconsistent chatter, it was the nocturnal revolution forged of silence and gentleness, but it was dangerous for writing was prophetic and we tended to realize its prophecies, even the darkest of them; and the paintings too that Florence thought she'd looked at with an indifferent eye in museums were, likewise, so often heavy with prophecies that Florence felt in herself that farewell to life and earth depicted by forms or colours; painters, young or old, women or men, united by an inspired expression monstrous with prophecy, had cried out in the silence of approaching catastrophe: "Beware, there will soon be war, calamities, look, look, it is coming, all the curses of the earth are at your door"; a portrait by Otto Dix representing a mother and child foretold for Florence that very decay: the mother and child were both famished, clasped in each others' arms on the point of death, and if they weren't going to die of their privations the grey hue of their faces, their chapped skin, already revealed them as survivors; sometimes that future, or this present, was seen sneaking up behind the figures in the paintings, as in Munch's painting of three young girls on a bridge surrounded by a river of fire; water was also a prophetic element, as his delirious mind had envisioned and painted it in *The Hamburg Deluge*, and this delirium came back to Florence with all the powers of her lucidity for she hadn't forgotten, perhaps, she thought, she had even read the history of the world in paintings, in images, while others, like Lucia and her family, had endured the whole sordid story of their lives without feeling sorry for themselves for such was their destiny, and thinking still about all that the image had taught her, a painting — she didn't know who had painted it, perhaps an unknown artist — remained in her memory: it was a small red house at the end of a grey street, there was nobody in the painting, just a terrible silence like the one surrounding Mike's chair; a threat hovered there, a presentiment, yes, it was almost nothing, and at that instant nothing seemed more threatening to her or heavier with prophecy than that silent grey street abandoned by men, and as for the little red house with closed shutters its mystery seemed akin to the one she had left behind her, behind the hermetically closed drapes of her house, all seemed to be silence and premonition there, you didn't know what would happen in such places, like in the interior of the red house with its closed shutters, it was a sign of flight, of exile, of deportation, and death had all that silence for itself, all that silence, she thought, and then Mike came back towards her saying, "Quick, Mom, some coffee for the lady we don't know, she's going to collapse on the stairs"; Gloria poured some whisky into Florence's coffee, saying, "We're used to troubles, ma'am, we've had more than our share in the family, what's wrong? Why don't you go upstairs and rest, the kids must bother you here...." No troubles, Florence said, straightening up proudly, none at all; she told herself she might have time to observe Mike, but he said, as he had said the first time he'd come to her on the stairs, "Drink it while it's hot." "Don't you go to school?" asked Florence. "No, not now, my mother and I we're getting ready to go to San Francisco, we're going to buy a new motorcycle." "Yeah," said Gloria, "thanks to my daily show at the *Infini* — no sex, kid, no bike. If it's your husband you're waiting for, ma'am, he'll come back, you shouldn't let yourself get so upset over a man, they all come back, but too late." Florence said she wasn't waiting for anything or anybody, you could empty yourself of all hope, all expectation, yes, such things did happen, and the stray cat was still following Berthe Agneli, for he wouldn't try to cross the bridge, what was the use of losing your blood, your life there, his heart had not yet had its fill of grass and of wind, no, this provisional existence pleased him — you were born, you disappeared, an ephemeral creature, it would have been futile to take time out for sadness, today you were alive, tomorrow you were dead; his path would be luminous, he had no lodgings, no bowl of milk in sight yet but he could race along the currents of the air, feeling the thrill of the unknown, while the bridge, the highway, signified the commotion of sudden deaths, of humiliating death-agonies, no, there were too many dead hopes on the bridge, and he went on, went on, his nostrils dilating towards the trees, the flowers, the sky, his paradise; John had said to Lucia, "My father's at the office, come on over to the apartment, we'll smoke some hash, watch baseball on TV, *peace and love, yes,*" both of them stretched out on their stomachs on the soft rug, they no longer looked at each other, fastened to the screen, "It's not bad," said John, "a nice feeling"; his parents were divorced, he would see his mother on his seventeenth birthday, he said slowly, dreamily, "If you do all they want, see, they pay you more, it depends..." but at that moment, sprawled in front of the television, sex seemed like such an unpleasant business and he had the feeling that his body trembled with disgust at the very thought of it; they remained still, unmoving, close to each other; it was strange, thought Lucia, that John, who lived off prostitution, opened up this zone of peace and chastity to her, offering her rest, the immobility of their two bodies, maybe she wouldn't be so afraid in his presence, John, an only son, a roomy apartment, a house, a lake in the country though John never went there, he had sold his last birthday present, a typewriter, for a bit of delirium, he did not like love, often it wasn't necessary, the needle had left its obscure ravages all over his emaciated flesh; maybe one should keep one's body all to oneself, what did Lucia think, "I don't know, I don't know," only pretend to give, and cut out at the right moment.... Lucia listened, she had a sister at the university and she herself hardly even knew her grammar, maybe Berthe was superior, the family wouldn't have shown such scorn for her if she hadn't been, and Lucia said to John, "As for Jojo, we'll keep her in school a long time — all the rest, topless and all that, it's all shit. . . . " John stretched out on his back and contemplated the ceiling, "a nice feeling", but Lucia didn't share John's euphoria, she didn't like hash and it seemed to her that the ceiling was going to slide down and crush the life out of her, with John and his untouchable body in its shell, a carnal shell she would have qualified as "transparent" in her present state of terror. Gloria gave Florence one of the ironic, probing looks that were famil- iar to the men who knew her: "When you leave off expecting anything, you pass over to the other side, you're no longer on our side of life, as long as you breathe you're killing yourself waiting for someone, something, . . . " then, without a glance at Mike who was standing beside her, Gloria took him by the hand and led him to the kitchen, as if to spare him the bitterness of her own thoughts, "And you, back on the job, boy, or we'll never get off on that trip, . . . " silence fell all around Florence once again and she told herself, "Gloria's right, I'm still breathing because I'm waiting for him, because I'm still here"; hadn't she been waiting for this mysterious delay to be over ever since her meeting with Judith Lange, waiting for the decision of the murderous thing she carried deep inside herself, which was slow in blossoming; if she liked museums, deserted train stations, empty, sunny streets, it was because her wait required these blank spaces, they were sanctuaries that allowed her fear a place to breathe; and yet during these speechless days of arrested fright no voice arose from within her — her thoughts stagnated or became fixed in her silence — and at the same time she distinctly heard all the other voices, they struck her like a foreign note that might shatter everything, often it was a voice that came and went leaving no trace, but now, on the stairs, she suddenly recalled a conversation she had overheard nearby, perhaps it had taken place behind her back, in one of those places where she'd thought she was alone: a grey-haired woman, her eyes shaded by dark glasses, had said to her husband, "I told Bernard not to leave, I was sure I'd never see him again if he left, but you refused to understand...." Florence had barely taken note of the grey hair and the fleeting look behind the shadow of the glasses; the man was probably close by, sitting to his wife's left, you could feel him there, immense and silent beside the woman, but you also felt that he wouldn't say anything, and what would Florence ever know about Bernard's tragedy, Bernard of whom she knew nothing except that a woman, his mother maybe, at his father's side, had just announced in a voice dried up by emotion and imponderable anger that he would never come back; where was he, why would he never come back, she wouldn't have time to find out for the couple was about to disappear in the direction of a train and their destination would remain invisible to her like Bernard's mysterious departure or arrival — if that incident in which, like so many others, she'd played no part suddenly came to mind, it was because she could still feel that particular silence falling around her, the man's vast, agitated silence, and because she remembered that after what had seemed a long time, a minute perhaps, the man had let out a low whistle; it wasn't, thought Florence, from lack of respect for his wife's pain but rather because under the circumstances he considered a whistle to be an appropriately cruel mockery of his own fate, of his powerlessness that was linked in this case to Bernard's destiny, to Bernard whom he had failed to understand, and henceforth his only certainty would be that Bernard would never come back. During the hours of impassive silence spent at John's side, Lucia wondered if life was only this rigid dance on the surface of things, this secret resistance, holding your ground and not dying of despair, John wasn't looking at her, from now on his look was closed, inviolable; nobody, not even Gloria who pretended to know all there was to know about Lucia, could have predicted just the day before that all these new feelings would surge up in her, nobody could have foreseen their blossoming in a girl who seemed so weightless and sensual, who had never been attracted by the ambiguity of doubt and fear; it was just that you couldn't predict anything, not even the return of habits that dispelled fear and doubt, and Lucia recalled all the burning days when she'd waited for Gloria at the door of the seedy places she frequented, places that exhaled all the city's emanations, its bandying and its wheedling — Gloria, her mother, was the goddess of those searing days, but now, thought Lucia, what a pitiful queen she was in that flesh market; or maybe she was like John who could make love all day long without ever offering his face, maybe he didn't even have one in love, and maybe love, for John as for Gloria, was present as a liberating function only, with its own silent mechanisms; their bodies stirred, tuned to their own volcanic activity, but the eruption of nerves and blood flung far from itself all that pertained to their heads and faces — far from thought, from the understanding of gestures and of the body — they themselves had chosen this exile, this separation of body and spirit; and like John they wandered in the limbo of this silence that some compared to the first thresholds of death, but who knows, Lucia thought, maybe John had a face she didn't know, that nobody had yet brought to life, a face that lay frozen elsewhere, in the intermittent pleasures that made up his life... all those days waiting for Gloria in the flaming city, Gloria was robed in the emanations of decay and of her innumerable seductions, of the steaming, battered city she lived in; this kind of sexual voracity, this open frantic expression of lust, Gloria said, should yield its weight in gold and glory instead of bringing you to defamation and misery; and as Lucia wandered on her own, waiting for her mother in the hot, hysterical city, she discovered the rules of the game, and this child of Gloria and her sisters strolled and laughed under the city's ardent roof; on scorching, corrupt nights they feasted, gathering around a table laden with pizzas and Cokes, the little girls in white sleeveless dresses, naked beneath the flimsy nylon, painted and powdered, but you could sense the paleness of malnutrition beneath the make-up, no, she, Lucia, wasn't like them at all, it was better to filch one of Mike's jackets, a pair of jeans, above all not to look like them. "I can sit down with you girls, *I am in business,* ... " his name was Dmitri, he shared their racial and linguistic confusion, a mongrel like Lucia, "born right here, like you girls, but in the business like the father I never saw... " then they asked him, "How do you peddle girls when your pretty mug's already scarred by so many knives?" and he stared into the distance, like John, blind and faceless, the body separated from the head, Lucia thought, somehow you read in his liquid blue eyes that he was just passing through, and the scar on his cheek remained engraved in Lucia's memory as the stamp of his weakness and suffering. Maybe that was the way it would all end, thought Lucia, maybe one day she'd be very old and would die of disgust, but none of them, not Gloria, nor John, nor Dmitri would know anything about it, or perhaps she'd be very old and so prosperous that they'd all be there, melting at her feet like candy in the sun; her thoughts were wandering, close to the smooth surface of John's face, to Dmitri's gaping look, push all this emptiness away, confine it to the limits of eternity, never again see them or breathe in the stagnant perfume of their flesh — but then it wasn't always like that, for John, like Dmitri, could also smell good in those hours of the night when the city was so close and so warm; at such times they didn't smell of dead roses or of stale kitchens as they did now, no, all of a sudden they gave off a heady odour, it was the taste of their youth, of their bodies, you could almost touch it, it was the airy substance of their exciting virility, of their awkward beauty — Gloria's children were arid and yet they'd been conceived in voluptuous distress, Luigi, Gloria and all the others, no, Judith Lange wouldn't come today, thought Mike, "She's your *sweetheart,* hé," said Gloria, setting her strong hand on Mike's shoulder, "hé, *love,* tell me the truth now, you got no cause to blush like that. . . ." Judith had spoken to her students of Hölderlin's elegies and now they were walking beside her under the canopy of white lilacs, but Langenais, as Anne Dupré called her, pushed them off gently, yes, Stuttgart is beautiful, "If a worry ties you in knots, put it aside for winter," a voice said, and Judith noticed Anne Dupré near her, "you don't like anybody, tell the truth, I feel it, you can't put anything over on me," Anne Dupré's voice went on, "No, you don't like me, Langenais, who could you possibly like, and yet I'm the brightest student in this college full of idiots and you know it..." and you must be very lonely, Judith Lange heard, but maybe she'd only imagined it for Anne Dupré added, "There's a boy who tried to commit suicide this morning, by fire. I know that kind of gesture touches you..." said Anne with a ferocious gleam in her eye; what right did Judith Lange have to like only misfortune, Anne didn't understand what right she had, Langenais never responded when you longed for tenderness, why did she back off from all sensual or verbal conflagrations, why did she keep herself far from the path of love, and its power over people? Maybe she feared that very dislocation of her secret, creative self, thought Anne Dupré, but that self was so secret that when you were with her you couldn't tell if you were sick with rage, or dazzled, or indignant at so much cruelty — Judith had a kind look, she was always attentive, why did she always avoid the cutting analysis that was Anne Dupré's privilege, and Judith Lange said, "I want to be alone...." "Always alone, oh, I understand," said Anne, at once defiant and undecided, and it seemed to her that Judith Lange moved without her in a forbidden circle, a hell that was Judith's alone, although if those zones she kept to were infernal how could she be in such a serene, kindly mood all the time? She'd spoken of poets and philosophers whose untimely deaths were due to the exhaustion of overly vigorous minds, but she herself was healthy, she was glad to be alive, why wouldn't she let herself be approached? It was also possible, thought Anne Dupré, that Judith was unaware of the instinct that guarded her against the torture of feelings, but that instinct was so strong that it preceded her everywhere, rigorously defending her against our intrigues, our trivialities; Anne no longer knew how to explain or condemn it, she turned back to her companions, but nothing seemed true or real in their company, they were self-satisfied in the afternoon light that was a prelude to rest, to the summer vacation, the crowning of a normal academic year, the kind of existence that would wear you out in the long run, would ruin you and in time become nothing more than enslaving trivialities and intrigues; but couldn't Judith's reserve be compared to Mike's, for he always seemed to give so very little of himself, it had troubled Florence quite a bit at first, when he had set the plate of burned spaghetti on her knees, issuing his order in a cutting tone: "Eat it while it's hot, my mother says so"; was it timidity, or respect for the life he would leave behind him, the fear of disturbing life in a moment of splendour or peace, that made him behave that way, or was it the presentiment that he would before long have to separate himself from the radiant intimacy he had dreamed of sharing with another person, when all the others, tomorrow and the day after, would draw closer and closer to each other, even Gloria and Tim who were always quarrelling, yes, life's small failures were but games compared to the victory of death; death — it alone could be called a certainty, like the departure of that unknown boy, Bernard, and thus Mike, pursuing his dialogue with death as Judith pursued hers with those who came back up from the suicidal abyss, no longer aspired to that delicious harmony with someone whose very breath, for his greater happiness, would have been music to him; the music he heard came from himself, it was the contrite lullaby he sang to himself in an empty room, some mischievous murmur that still triumphed over his revolt — for the dying never weary in their struggle, and after all, who among us could reconcile the explosion of life with the obliteration of death? — and Mike held on stubbornly, resisting as his ancestral instinct taught him to for it wasn't in keeping with his dignity to just peter out and submit, and though the agonies of death might become atrociously long drawn out, deciding to belong to yourself to the very end was a demented, sacred thing, Florence thought, but if only, if only he would look at me, come a bit closer, yes, I'd be able to see him better, to imagine the existence of a person like him, but he wouldn't understand. "What a strange girl Langenais is," thought Anne Dupré, laughing quietly, Anne Dupré, twenty years old, refusing passivity, striking, with dazzling determination and will-power, that's who I am — one look at me and they'll understand, I have no time to lose, I know what I want, everything, there have been too many generations of submissive sheeplike women, if she wants to be a loner, O.K., I'll be an even greater loner than she is . . . they were asking her if she had liked the class, "I was afraid it would bore me, but you're never bored with Langenais, she makes you suffer too much . . ." Anne said, laughing; they listened to you, looked at you with admiration, they always listened to Anne Dupré when she spoke, but there was no danger of these ignorant little students commanding her emotions —sometimes, when she felt like it, she would take one home with her, always with the look of authority that shocked and overwhelmed them; Judith had spoken of the balance of terror between life and death, that balance these days, thought Anne, is called sexual desire, Langenais is a romantic who has somehow strayed into our century, she talks to us about victims but I can't stand all that, you have to learn to defend yourself in this life—what an odd professor, this summer I can go to Mexico, alone or with a friend, write my autobiography while she'll probably spend the summer with her victims and her survivors of history—you've got to be crazy, degenerate, there are still sheeplike women around even these days, sex is that balance without terror, but that simply hasn't ever occurred to her; it's spring, the sap is rising, I'm going to go out tonight, I won't come back in the fall if she isn't teaching here. . . . "Tell me, Mickey," said Gloria, "just what we'll see in the desert, you and I." "The Indians," he began, "used to say that some of the plants are poisonous —there's the cactus, the indigo bush that cures you, desert lavender and honey, and a plant called white sage that defends you against curses, according to the Indians." "We'll go into the desert and we'll brew a mixture of all those plants and you'll be feeling better in three days' time, Mickey. . . . " Florence glimpsed the outline of a smile on his lips but it vanished at once, for Charlie's silhouette had invaded the narrow space where Mike and Gloria were standing close together conquered by the innocence of their dream, like two people immobilized in an embrace that cuts them off from the world. "Now what have you done to have the police on your tail?" asked Gloria when she became aware of Charlie panting behind her. "A bank job our gang screwed up," said Charlie, "all I want is to go back to prison, yeah, so they just lock me up and be done with it!" "In that case, beat it, you damn bum," said Gloria, "that way I'll have more steak for my kids, you rotten thief!" Gloria didn't usually remain silent when Charlie went to prison — the sight of a man humiliated, handcuffed, going off with his head bowed, didn't please her at all, but this time there were no wails, no cries, Mike noticed, and it worried him that violence should suddenly disappear from his life this way; maybe Gloria was just too worn out to get angry, or maybe she hoped to see the young murderer again who'd been accused of rape, but Mike was afraid — wasn't it a sign that even his mother who had always seemed invincible foresaw that she would soon be dominated, vanquished, and this time it was Mike who felt Charlie's humiliation when they came to get him, what would happen to him, how would they treat him, would he ever see him again, after all, he was just a man hard-hit by misfortune, "Mom, don't let him go yet, tell him to wait. . . . " "Wait for what, Mickey? I'm not the one who brought that coward into the world. . . don't give me that look, they'll take him away and good riddance to him, O.K., go back to your own business, look after Jojo, don't get mixed up in this. . . . " There would be more of this emptiness, this absence, and the dogs would wail alone in the yard at night, more of that slow anguish that some-times lasted until dawn, when Luigi slept so soundly with an angelic curl to his lips, but the cactus, the indigo bush that cures, the desert lavender and honey, maybe none of it was true, the desert soil was fragile, the wind uprooted everything overnight, the desert dust was burning hot and Judith Lange wouldn't come today, the other woman was still sitting on the stairs, still watching him, she was neither hungry nor thirsty, what was she waiting for, she seemed exhausted but from time to time he felt her burning look on him — yes, maybe none of it was true, the only sure thing was that Charlie would go to prison because he wasn't comfortable here in this urban desert where he did nothing but wait for his sentence. "Don't worry," Gloria said, "we'll go see him on Sundays just like in the good old days, that's what life is all about, Mike, the same things keep happening over and over again...." Charlie walked so softly that Florence barely noticed when they came to take him away, Charlie, she heard a low voice say, Charlie, and he went off with a stupefied gait, two grey men holding him by the arm like a convalescent, silently, silently, maybe that was the way one left life, all wrapped up in that tranquil stupor, the voices around us suddenly stilled; she recalled her conversations with Judith — it seemed strange to her that the girl had seized so much of the past, as though she'd preceded Florence in life, Florence thought; unlike herself, Judith believed that nothing around us was lost — when she visited a Monument to the Dead in a European city it straightway began to press upon her memory, and she saw, there where so many saw nothing, a river of blood, the ghost of all the blood that had been spilled haunted her and yet she was in no way to blame, those crimes had been committed before her birth,

or perhaps, thought Florence, Judith incarnated other
beings, the souls of those who hadn't understood why they
were being flung into the abyss and who had asked on the
threshold of death, "Will my executioners be punished
one day, or will you entertain the illusion that the world
will one day be better? Or will you just forget?" She bore
the weight of souls who refused to forget or to let
themselves be wiped out by the executioner's forgetful-
ness, and, yes, thought Florence, maybe that's why the
pages of the book of suffering — often closed to those who
live and suffer, for the effervescence of the present leads
them to forget the bloody opacity of the past, even makes
them forget part of the present — were open to Judith; and
her fault lay in the fact that she knew how to read this
infinitely cruel book in which all our wrongdoings, even
those crimes so shameful that no amount of repentance
can ever redeem them, were inscribed, stamped on our
flesh for all eternity; but she wants to live, and why, when
all I want to do is die, if I were like Charlie I'd be safe,
tonight I'd be able to tell myself: the door is locked, I can
no longer run away, commit any threatening act, act
furtively against myself, shut in, captive, I can no longer
attempt those acts that are our undoing; "Well, that's that,
I'll come to see you with the boy one of these Sundays,"
Gloria said, "in the meantime you'll have a free supper
every night but you won't have me, your pearl, oh no,
you'll be sleeping with your fleas, and with your boys
when you get to feeling really lonely, you've my permis-
sion to do anything you want. . . ." Living alone, no longer
waiting for night, thought Gloria, one man or another, the
dream is over, "Mike, you'd better think about getting

ready for the trip before too long, don't you think?" she said. "I'm going to buy you some coloured T-shirts, nothing but coloured ones, that way they'll be brighter in the sun and I want you to be the handsomest of them all. . . ." "First we have to buy a suitcase, Mom," Mike said, "we don't have anything to pack stuff in yet." "You're right, a suitcase, I hadn't thought of it, but you're right, you might even say it's the essential thing, kid, no suitcase, no departure. . ." and as Gloria and Mike continued talking about the trip, celebrating once more the idea of taking off, of life in motion, another of those voices that had cried out in the anonymous crowd in which she'd taken refuge so often came back to Florence: it was a Greek waiter telling a client he was attending to with great dignity, "Oh, yes, sir, *born an immigrant and I'll die an immigrant. . . .* " The words were so simple — I was born in a foreign country and one of these days I'll die in a foreign country — so precise, and their particular ring was suddenly vibrating in her, isolated from the rest, she was besieged by the space and silence of a man born elsewhere, who had come from elsewhere and who was going to die elsewhere, although, young as he was, death was probably a long way off; all of a sudden she understood what it all meant, it was the cry of a man alone, and thinking of the lullaby Mike sang to himself she heard that muffled call, the barely audible call of solitude, it rose silently from afar, and there was often irony for oneself in those words, in those voices that had remained silent for so long, for the plight of the immigrant as they told it was often the story of our own destitution in this world; like Florence, the Greek waiter had lost his country at birth, his native country's song was now just a diffuse echo in time, and occasionally, when he'd had too much to drink, he could be seen mimicking his country's music, tapping out a silent, folkloric effusion on the tabletops, he closed his eyes, gave himself over as if in prayer to the contemplation of a world whose nostalgic fragments still haunted him, but that world would never return, thought Florence, and so it was that all these moments of unalterable beauty passed before our eyes, mocking and cruel: the smile, the look of a man who had charmed and seduced you, the ideal world that he created around himself in order to please you more or immobilize you in that seduction, it was all far away among those dead comets that still flashed through our memories, for memory was an instrument of possession, a caged creature that nevertheless wielded unlimited powers in its game of torture, in its power to possess us and to possess others too through remembrance, and this was so very true, thought Florence, that if it hadn't been for her faculty of recall — that ate away at her constantly, heavy with all her changing, capricious pasts — if it hadn't been for her memory, wouldn't she have decided to put an end to her days before then? As it was, this faculty for feeling and seeing once again and with total lucidity what she'd previously experienced, preserved life and the desire to live in her, even if it was only out of curiosity; for memory also conferred upon us the ability to wonder, to be astonished, however violent the despair. Lucia asked John, "Why don't we go up north, the two of us, we could hide out in the woods or go swimming, we'd be all alone, . . ." a house in the country, for John who never went there, a lake — his father, a dentist, had bought an island somewhere, he went there with his mistress, John said, staring, detached and distant, at the ceiling; his adventures had carried him so far away that he couldn't imagine himself suddenly sharing the adolescence of the rich boys he'd grown up with, alone in the middle of them all, whimsical and rebellious, summer would come, he felt only disgust for those languid summers at the lake that meant the company of relatives and friends, spoiled children sliding over the sleepy water in their boats each evening, playing in the sun during the day, their slender bodies conveying vague desires he couldn't understand when it was so easy to pierce the mystery of life, when there was no mystery; nor could he understand those students who took off for James Bay, falling victim to the illusions of fortune when all the fortune you had you carried in yourself, why work sixty hours a week at James Bay when sex offered such simple, tireless paths, summer lasted barely three months and they were imprisoned up north, toiling in a savage, rocky nature, crouching on a level with the caribou moss under the black spruces, they were mercenaries, John thought, in those vast, often blighted spaces, the trees refused to grow there so what kind of despair or greed could push men to go there? "We could swim right across the lake," said Lucia, "or go fishing," but she could see she was boring John—the house, the lake were no longer part of his world, she couldn't evoke the scenes she'd only known in dreams, and Lucia wondered how she could exchange her life for another; yes, thought Florence, it was possible that Judith Lange had been among us for a very long time, that was why she couldn't resign herself, she knew too much, like

Florence she too had the faculty of recall but her memories weren't personal ones, all she remembered was the oppression inflicted by strangers; it was a shame to sacrifice your youth to that ideal and above all it was useless, but we are often the sole makers of our misfortunes, thought Florence, they stem from ourselves and from our alienation from all that we have cherished on earth, from dreams of egoism and triumph, those dreams we had hoped to realize alone or with another person; from now on her own dream was cut off from the man she had loved, her dream had reduced her to a chronic state of crumbling; those who looked life's realities straight in the eye seemed to survive that kind of downfall but Florence preferred not to be cured for recovery would have obliged her to start all over again, to live on a level of slowness and despondency that she could no longer face. Madame Langenais paced the empty house with its blue drapes, turned the record over for Gilbert, yes, that's right, she came and went, contemplated the size of her home, but this house is much too big, I should speak to the children about it, Charles and I are getting on in age, why not sell everything, rent an apartment closer to the centre, or perhaps Charles would consider taking a sabbatical; I've always longed to go to Vienna, Gilbert, the maid, all the cares of daily life, why didn't she and Charles go out for dinner from time to time the way they used to when he was a student, what did that French woman say to her friend the other night, I hardly heard, sparks of conversation, Charles always tells me I'm tactless, "During the 1940 exodus, my baby came down with whooping cough, we had taken in some Belgian refugees . . . we saved him by a miracle, a chance meeting with the director of a sanatorium,..." the exodus, the baby, whooping cough, the woman was my age, thought Madame Langenais, but I haven't lived at all, not yet, Judith talks about people who can no longer change because it's too late — oh! she'll see, to begin with we'll have to sell this house, it's too big, no, that woman was marked by another destiny, but who cares, she endured the exodus and during those trying times her baby came down with whooping cough, how would she herself have behaved under similar circumstances, Judith, her eldest, had been spared the exodus, and yet it was as if the other woman had succeeded in spite of everything where Madame Langenais had failed, for today the child they had miraculously saved was a contented young man, satisfied with life, while Judith, Judith.... Madame Langenais shrugged her shoulders with an injured look; as a mother she felt disappointed, withered, the Bach cantata, the beauty of the world, I hope Charles won't decide to come home too early, of course all that took place elsewhere, on another continent, and yet you'd never guess when you came across that greedy woman in a restaurant, treating herself to fine wine and filet mignon, there was no visible trace of the sinister past — even those who endured such things must forget, we are oblivion's territory, and Charles and I, we might also be on vacation all the time, in love with each other; all they're concerned with is having fun, they don't give their schoolwork as much attention as they ought to, what will become of them without their mother, but Judith, she's different, she never needed us or not enough at any rate, but her sisters don't have her intelligence fortunately — how unbearable it would be as a mother to be outclassed, misunderstood by each of them, but oh! she's in for a surprise, the girl doesn't really know who I am, she doesn't know Josephine, her mother! How had it happened, wondered Monsieur Langenais, lost in his thoughts before the patch of tulips, how was it that he hadn't seen the group of children on roller skates bearing down on him? They had rolled down towards him, their arms raised towards the sky like arcs, they'd barely brushed him in their unbroken descent, maybe it was just the surprise that had thrown him off balance; he'd managed to grab hold of a tree but suddenly his glasses — or rather what remained of them — were at his feet, tiny glass slivers whose sharp edges seemed to challenge him like the teeth of an angry mouth, and in the distance one of the children called to his friend, "Be careful, we almost knocked an old man down...." Had anyone ever referred to him in such offending terms? "An old man..." — it was so impolite, what would they say twenty years from now when he was a defenceless old man? He was always solicitous of children, especially his own, but now, while brushing the dust from his coat, he regretted the "old times" his wife spoke about, and as he bent over to recover the fragile object that had come to such a sudden end, the brilliant pieces of glass gathering the light of day against the rough grey sidewalk struck his imagination like signs or omens: he'd never lost his balance, not even when he was hiking in the mountains, nobody had ever called him an "old man" — the nurses at his clinic did observe, among themselves, that he was "well preserved", and even that pharmaceutical expression rather shocked him but he definitely preferred it to "old man". Maybe Judith was right when she said he was too sentimental, that his life lacked firmness, why all of a sudden was the thought of these slivers of glass so afflicting? It was only a slight shock, a passing vertigo, he considered himself to be at the peak of his life, but all the same, were these portents not a foreboding of weaknesses that lay in wait for him? I'm so short-sighted, I wonder how I'm going to make it home, it's a good thing I have a spare pair at home, they didn't even say they were sorry, one no longer excuses oneself these days...oh! it's so nice out, better to forget the whole thing, with all the miserable people in the world we have no cause to complain—healthy children, a marvellous wife, she's a bit difficult at times but, well, so I am becoming sentimental, and according to Judith that's not reality, but what reality is she talking about? Walking in the dark changes everything, everything, thank goodness I have another pair at home. At the Hôtel des Voyageurs, a young woman Gloria had never seen before came in suddenly and asked for a room for the night; her name was Frédérike, "Another preposterous name," said Gloria, "what brings you to our dangerous city, sweetheart, if I may ask?" "Mozart's mass, it's going to be sung tomorrow night, maybe you read about it in the papers? In the Anglican church, there, across the street...." "What do you know, I never noticed I had an Anglican church right in front of my eyes...it'll cost you about seven dollars...Mike, show our guest to number eight, she'll have a view of the park and the church there...." Frédérike passed by Florence without seeing her, her eyes lowered to the key-ring Mike had given her to hold while he wiped his hands on his apron as his mother had just advised him, "All I want is a room for the night, I only have ten dollars on me," Frédérike told Mike, the hotel seemed rather odd but Gloria had given her a good welcome, did Mike like music, no, he said, shrugging his shoulders with a sulky, sad look on his face, his own ignorance saddened him and music, like all the other things which in the future would comfort other people's lives, seemed futile to him, a negation of his dreams; Frédérike entered the room, Mike went down into the shadows of the kitchen, Florence heard his steps passing near her; curiosity, she thought, that antiquated sentiment that kept us awake to the very end, Frédérike was some unknown girl who'd spoken about a Mozart mass in this profane place, grey-blue eyes with rings under them but they hadn't been directed towards Florence; a virginal forehead crossed by an occasional wrinkle of worry above the childlike eyebrows, a thirteenth-century painter would have liked to paint that face, to reveal the metaphysical care that fleetingly troubled her eyes, before long Frédérike would come and sit on the stairs, her father a musician, two sisters violinists, didn't Florence like that Mozart mass, no, the trombone isn't a very subtle instrument, it's the herald of death, the voice of the Last Judgement, "but the feeling of fright is attenuated at the end of the work," Frédérike said, striking the air with her nervous hand. "My husband and I used to go to the Salzburg Festival," said Florence, "but I was a society woman and deaf to everything, you wouldn't understand, you look like you're still quite innocent...." "Look," Frédérike said, "it's written in the score, you can feel it, Mozart feared that grave, monotonous voice, it was his last work, he felt death approaching, but I must go back to my room, get some work done, is the boy who showed me to my room wounded? Why is his head bandaged?" "These things happen, misfortunes," Florence said, "life expels us and we fall down in pieces, but don't stay here with me, I'm boring. . . ." "Come to the concert tomorrow." "Yes, maybe I will if I'm feeling better," said Florence, and Frédérike disappeared, still awkward and nervous, her wavy hair covering her face that seemed to belong to another age; perhaps Mozart felt the grace of life for the last time when he composed that mass, thought Florence, the grace of life, when even in misfortune divinity seemed to be a smiling accomplice — perhaps he'd been inspired to write that music, not as a song of resignation but as a proud call to hope; Florence now recalled that she'd been blessed with that kind of grace in her misfortune but she hadn't responded — it was when she'd met Judith; the next day the grace had disappeared, making way for the empty train station, her suitcase dragging her down towards the ground, and that bloody stain on the stairs, it wasn't her blood, the memory of Judith Lange's words resounded in the deserted train station: the cement, the bricks, the stones, the whitewashed walls still bore the traces of those who had been afraid, the whitewash, the bricks, the stones still trembled with the buried steps of fear, you cannot forget anything, you could placidly con-template Egyptian pyramids and Greek temples for the silence of centuries had engulfed the voices of the slaves, and yet from time to time a cry of torture still escaped from those lips sealed by an eternal secret only we were so deaf we barely perceived it, and blood didn't fade, it followed us everywhere, the sight of it shocked us, punished us constantly; if the same Frédérike Florence had just admired, fresh and awkward in her summer dress, had been born elsewhere, a few decades earlier, she might have alighted from a funeral train to ask the same thing she had asked of Gloria upon entering the hotel — "But where am I?" — her soul chilled by the strains of Mozart's music that reached her ears, sung by the victims who had till then been spared. "But where am I?" She would have directed her question to the sky and the earth and then, without understanding why, she would have followed the others towards the small wood from which a column of black smoke could be seen rising; without understanding why, she would have lost her life there in the massacre's daily scramble, and who would have heard her voice or her scream? In the surrounding villages, they saw the black smoke rising towards the sky but they didn't hear the voice of torture, they had closed their shutters and they no longer set foot outside for the streets had become heavy with an unbearable silence and moreover the black smoke might have crossed your threshold, contaminated your children and your pets, it might have killed you like a plague; nor did they speak to each other any more, for somebody might have mentioned the black smoke that rose in the sky day and night, a human conflagration that seemed to blaze twenty-four hours a day with practically no resistance for it was happening in the distance, in the secret of eternal silence, they had learned to keep quiet, they no longer spoke, for that black smoke, malevolent as it was, might have sprung suddenly from your lips to betray the dead whose ashes floated nearby, the ashes the wind scattered in your garden, blew in under your door, yes, they knew all that and they were afraid; just a few decades before, in another country, Frédérike might have perished that way, innocently and without understanding why, as she followed the others towards the small wood where black smoke rose continuously, while voices sang Mozart's mass for her in the distance. There'll be the cactus, thought Mike, the indigo bush that cures, desert lavender and honey; maybe it will be a miniature desert, thought Mike, no bigger than the kitchen, with grass yellowed by summer winds and barely enough room to move or lie down, maybe the walls of the sky will close in on you, for death will be present everywhere, beneath the desert rose, under the grass and the fine sand, it'll come right up against the nape of your neck, it'll call and whistle in your ear with the intoxicating softness of the air, and while you pretend to play, while you run with Gloria, it will be watching close by, with the indigo bush that cures, the lavender and honey, at first it will hesitate, trying to find a crack through which it can worm its way into you; it will be strange to be there, all alone with this ultimate scenery of death expanding as far as the eye can see, calm, deep, and gentle, above all without anger in it; or perhaps the desert will be inhabited by a few men — a few men with dogs since for you must never set off without a companion — you will see them rise up and disappear into the blind, unfeeling blue sky, always accompanied, never alone, for their frail silhouettes might fade out in the treacherous air, they will go without stopping, without turning back to you, but you will see those black shapes that were their dogs dissolve slowly in the light, the memory of the companion and his bent shadow will walk behind you, for little by little the men walking in the desert will become no more than memories and shadows, and Mike thought yes, we'll go, soon, there will be the cactus, the indigo bush that cures, lavender and honey, and as he repeated the melody to himself he felt a presence in the bar, at his mother's side, a presence that was as dark and heavy as the obscure bulk of the police dogs that had followed him to the threshold of eternity; it was as if his terror had suddenly taken on a face, a form — the tranquil, shapeless hulk standing there might be called a man and yet it was a grotesque, unkempt thing that seemed to have swallowed all the air of the room in an instant. Even Gloria seemed frightened and cried out, "Hey, this one's come up from the caves!" and then she set a beer before him, observing the man with fascination, it was something avid and noisy and its bestial force encircled her and Mike knew that she wouldn't resist, tonight or tomorrow she'd shut herself up with the caveman, with that intransigent brutality, this hulk could gobble her up, enslave her, he knew she wouldn't resist, and he turned his head quickly towards Florence as if to say, "Can't you see my mother's in danger, why don't you help her?" but Florence didn't seem to see him and at that moment she appeared to Mike as the embodiment of inertia, she was the very indifference of those who were no longer willing to see or hear, her hands, knotted in anguish, were resting on her knees, her vision was shut in upon itself; he longed to tell her, "Look, we're still here, all around you — Gloria, my mother, and this man, a beast, at her side, and space is shrinking up around us"; you could hear the man breathing greedily in and out in the room, but Florence, absorbed in her icy dreaming, was apparently deaf to it all, her anguish in living was contained in the nervous movement of her hands, they were beautiful, useless hands, she thought, the hands of a marble effigy on a tomb, clenched from the labour of a sterile mind no longer touched by exaltation, reality was a rough stone, a cold, unmagical stone that collided with our fragile limbs, especially with our hands, they changed when they came into contact with it; thus we were transformed over the years, because of this rough, cold contact, we went along tying ourselves in knots, dwindling away, our dreams alone sparkled like diamonds in an internal night but they were weak, power-less dreams. Florence strained to cover all the fragments of her life that were breaking loose, she wondered if she'd had one or several faces for this husband who had known her so well during the flash of her life, perhaps she'd had none since he had chosen, in leaving her, to chastise every expression of happiness or hope those faces might have had; no face, no body, maybe she'd left no trace of her passage in that man's life, no perfume, and nothing could offend her more for he would never come back to say it, to prove that she'd had a refuge near him, he would never say it, he had even erased the memory of his tender words in this silence that annihilated everything, bringing fog in its wake; yes, a fog was descending upon her gradually, for she could no longer recall the unity of the face she'd loved, she remembered a banker they'd met together in Saigon, she remembered a Dublin poet she'd passed one day in a hotel lobby, but the harmony of that face she knew so much better than the others was suddenly broken up; she

saw the sandals she had found in the closet in a halo of
light, but what were his brown feet like, what translucent
haze was engulfing them bit by bit, or were they wandering, like so many others that nobody thinks about, that no
woman loves? Sometimes she thought that her love had
transformed itself into a hatred so great that she had begun
to forget it, that this haze descending slowly over her
dearest memories was nothing but the aura of a hatred she
could no longer contain, hatred, she thought, because he,
who was only a man, had taken on the retributive role of
destiny, he had determined the nature of her misfortune,
he had delivered her over to death without a word, and
she had discovered that this executioner who had inflicted
so many blows upon her, one by one, in silence, probably
obeyed a ritual that he himself didn't understand, for it is
perfectly natural to grow tired of a woman, a house, a son,
she thought, it's natural to tire of everything and disappear, the world is already so hostile, and nothing in it
compels us to assume, as a couple, that which overwhelms
us so when we're alone, we're under no obligation to shut
ourselves up in that often ill-fated and subterranean dual-
ity, except that such confinement of love and passion is
imperative and imposes its own laws and necessities;
nonetheless there was always a crack, an incision between
two lovers united by daily rhythms or the feverish impulse
that drew them together, there was always a threat
hanging over those heads so piously attentive to each
other; hatred, hatred, thought Florence, and hatred especially for all the illusions the image of the couple had
nurtured and encouraged for such a long time, and it
seemed to her that the guiltiest of these illusions was to

have believed that she would go through life without suffering when in fact she was now constantly plagued by unmeasurable suffering, by the agony of vacillating, doubting thought, when this suffering was going to cut her off from the world...and suddenly the image loomed before her, so cruel in its precision: as she'd seen the sandals in the closet, she now saw the absent fingers stroking hers, felt the thrilling caress along her fingers, leaving the mark of a boring day on her skin; it had been one of those days when one waited vaguely for something to happen, he'd reached for her hand out of idleness as they came back from the pool, had begun to toy with her fingers, and boredom, the monotony of the days, had slipped morbidly into the caress that seemed so light, so quick; at the time she'd had no idea how terrible the lazy invention of our gestures could become, she had surrendered her fingers, her hand, her arm to the caress and she could still feel its electricity running through her; others had maybe taken notice of it, had maybe been jealous of that apparently lasting, eternal complicity—who knows what suffering they'd inflicted upon the solitary witness who watched them, hatred, hatred, she scorned him for having perhaps lost his dignity at that very instant, with his bored, silent caress, for having lost what had been his only kingdom as well as the mystery of her mind that he'd never really understood, either because he was lacking curiosity or because he became bored too quickly in the company of women; "Poor Charlie," said Gloria with a sigh, and Mike didn't know how to interpret her doleful exclamation; the kitchen was Gloria's refuge from the tide of putrid men who drank in her looks, gulped down her breath all day long, it was

Mike's desert where lavender, and roses so fine that you only recognized them by their heady fragrance, would blossom some day; she approached him sighing, "Poor Charlie, he'll sleep alone tonight!" Poor Charlie, thought Mike, and she opened the window because the spring air was good for him, and soon he'd be breathing in the summer intoxication she was always telling him about, Jojo ran to the window, the pigeons, Stéphane, when would he come back, all the birds were back but Stéphane never came to play in the park any more accompanied by his blonde, slender mother, what would it be like in summer, thought Mike, when the grass in the park was already trampled, burnt, when the city was bubbling with a commotion that resounded in his nervous, imprisoned heart, what would it be like in summer, what would happen to us if rain and snow no longer came to quench our thirst beneath the sky that had remained so implacably blue for the past few days already; preparations for the summer they were all waiting for had already begun, people were cleaning up the city, filling in the gaping wounds left by winter, a young worker with a black beret was sweating in the sun, deep down in one of those holes that in just a few hours would become a trench or a road, the rough-surfaced buildings climbed up towards the sky while he descended, descended, his absurd shovel scraping away at the asphalt and the cement, sometimes assisted by a monstrous machine that would have ground him to a pulp in its steel jaws if he hadn't possessed an innate athletic alertness that protected him in consciousness' stead, in winter and summer one could glimpse the worker and his black beret down in the hole, lost against the indifferent height of the sky, digging his trench; when would he climb back up into daylight, and when would deliverance come, Mike wondered while his mother kept repeating, "Poor Charlie, poor Charlie," the worker's bare back was already reddened by the sun, tomorrow he would be shivering with cold; Mike moved away from the blazing window; was the underground trench as narrow as their tiny kitchen, did silence come buzzing in your ear there, Gloria's silence, Florence's silence as she sat on the stairs, the silence of all these disappointed people who were like a wall around him, Gloria, Charlie, Lucia who came home late every night until the moment arrived when she wouldn't come home any more, neither in the evening nor at night; none of them would be granted even a fleeting moment of regeneration or hope during his life's brief season, he thought, for life destroyed life, and wasn't that the only thing you really understood during your passage on earth? All the same, thought Florence, was it not strange to feel that hatred when so many still considered love to be a certainty, perhaps the only certainty? All those happy couples filed past in her memory, they came from all walks of life, they composed the universe and gave it warmth, until then she'd never noticed to what extent they all demonstrated the same egoism or to what extent their insolent likeness to each other set them apart from other people's misfortunes; men or women, two by two they established a cell of desire and contradictions that made them suddenly appear as indistinguishable, indivisible matter in the eyes of drifting humanity: they had been two atoms, love or passion had accomplished the stormy fusion, yes, it would last a while or forever, this victorious

atom with its indissoluble purity, and the lovers, all drunk
with the same hope, went their way, ignoring everything
that wasn't themselves, you couldn't take your eyes off
them but they took no notice of anyone; Florence recalled
two young women, ice-skaters she'd seen quarrelling in a
sports centre—one of them had too much pride and
vitality to give in to the other's stubbornness—and yet, in
spite of the angry shouts, the young skaters made up one
uncompromising whole, each of them held the promise of
happy tomorrows and the reminiscence seemed all the
more bitter since it was associated in Florence's mind with
her husband's caress, with the bored, silent atmosphere
that had just begun to exist between them, they never
quarrelled like the two young skaters, they didn't speak,
and not long after that caress she had walked around in an
unfamiliar city, it was a comfortable city and she felt good
there, she might come across a museum where she could
pass the rest of the afternoon for she had a sudden need to
bring each day to a conclusion without a glance at what
might follow, and the skaters had appeared, their skates
dangling from their shoulders, one of them dressed in
white, the other in red, they were unpolished, ardent, and
beautiful, she'd looked at them as if stunned, moved
without understanding why for she hadn't had time to
reflect upon the tragic, heavy sense of the caress along her
hand, the terminal caress perhaps, she couldn't say, not
yet, but she knew that that long day had to come to a
close, had to cease being, and the skaters' voices were
shrill, their words rash and sometimes vulgar, they were
alive—love, rage, indignation were living feelings, all this
belonged to an order of life, to a secret harmony, and yet

nothing could seem more disorderly, more unpredictable than such an attachment, such an attraction that bound two beings together; belonging to that hidden, inexorable order of life defied the laws of reason, Florence thought, and yet the reality of the couple became perfectly symmetrical once one had penetrated its contents, its qualities and shortcomings, but you could only understand all that, she thought, once you were on the outside, once the couple had agonized and succumbed, you could understand it only when it was no longer a tangible reality and had become a mere ghost, when it seemed nothing more than a sleek, miserable facet of our life on earth; and yet the skaters were still there, triumphing together over the difficulties of solitary life that Florence still had to face alone, triumphing over the bitterness of her reflections, triumphing over everything; it was summer, the city was a comfortable one, and the sight of the skating rink sparkling in its huge glass cage heightened the feeling of strangeness and solitude Florence had felt that same day when she'd asked herself, "But where am I?" She was right there on earth where she'd always been, but she abruptly found herself at the edge of an unidentifiable precipice, it was going to happen, he hadn't said anything but it was coming, he would leave her, it wouldn't be long now, maybe he'd go without a word, and the skaters, who had stopped quarrelling, were speeding around the glass cage, around the skating rink covered over with translucent gold, it all belonged to them, it was their space to play in, they were an unpredictable, luminous couple, but there was something even less predictable than that couple, thought Florence, and that was the suffering caused by the

knowledge that they were, like herself, women; she had
always considered loving her sole moral guide in life, and
now she had suddenly had a glimpse of a joyous, amoral
territory that everyone, herself excepted, could conquer,
and she'd wished that that kind of happiness might be
outlawed or at least that she might become blind to these
activities in which she could now have no part; since the
skaters were like Florence they too might one day have to
endure the unspeakable torture she'd seen foreshadowed
as she strolled in the city, but today they were triumphant,
maybe they would still be so tomorrow while Florence
would return to the torment of meaningless caresses and
feigned embraces, to silence, the silence of women that
was hers, but what hurt Florence was that the skaters
weren't suffering, quite the contrary: their appearance
alone could still be compared to hers, to her biological
existence — they breathed and slept like herself but their
sleep was relaxed and sublime while Florence had the
impression she would never again sleep that kind of sleep,
that from then on she would only descend and descend,
sinking straight down, the weight of the silence dragging
her down towards a troubling place of unfathomable
depths and unknown, suspicious revelations. Florence had
been unexpectedly invaded by a horror of level country-
sides and of calm smooth seas; she had the feeling that that
kind of topographic neutrality would poison her life with
dangerous dullness, the very dullness that stoked the fire
that ravaged her in her husband's presence; you had to
take off for greater altitudes, it was a matter of life or
death, and yet everything conspired to drag you back
down; why not take off for Nepal, for the Himalayas

whose summits bowed to the masterful forces of money and tourists' curiosity — she would thus find herself in the vicinity of a strong, warring world, of the rock *par excellence*, of cold, of absence, and lofty evasion, vainly acquiescent; above all, she'd be accompanied neither by him nor by the memory of his humiliating caress, it would be her first trip without him, in the indiscriminate motion of the world which would skim over her pain without depriving her of the proud suffering she could sustain deep down inside; how lamentable it all seemed when she considered that that striving for greater altitudes which had appeared from the inside to represent total evasion, which had had the crystalline quality of a dream, would terminate here at the Hôtel des Voyageurs between Gloria and Mike, in a hole you couldn't climb out of, for either there were no walls, no sides to it, or else they'd been ripped apart so that any desire to scale them and go somewhere else was vain; and yet she'd begun to feel, all the same, that she was in her place here; if God existed it undoubtedly pleased Him to see her here rather than elsewhere, but she would have liked to share that dream with Mike, to tell him about the vision of the Himalayas she'd carried in her heart in other times, how it would have pleased her to tell him all about it, to entrust him with this dream she'd had of discovering a new taste for life, omitting what had ensued — the disappointing reality, bitterness, and disgust which now drowned out even the world's greatest beauties; maybe she could reach through to Mike, she thought, but it was too late, he listened smilingly when Gloria spoke to him about the desert but death had already robbed him of it, death was present and he was no longer anything but a deaf child in the city; perhaps Mike, with this evil he never mentioned eating away at him in silence, would have shared with Florence the disenchantment, the weariness that follows feverish hopes, and she longed to put the exclusive, grandiose world that seemed to have been created for the sole pleasure of the rich and powerful within Mike's reach, before his eyes that eluded the light; but it was too late now that the fog was descending all around her and all these treasures she would never see again were obscured by night, and she recalled that when she had found herself all alone, when she had sensed that the man's impending departure was about to cut her off from everything around her, she had been able to identify herself with that colossal nature so often barren in its splendour and so cold that it could be compared only to ourselves when we reached a certain state of deprivation and rigidity, although its coldness surpassed ours for nature knew no anguish and remained immobile and impassive and observed us as we were, without motion or subtlety. Yes, Florence could compare herself to the summits of those barren mountains, to that whiteness gazing into emptiness, she was like the starkest glaciers, like them she was learning to remain unmoving, calm, uncaring, and the man separated himself from her gradually like a continent afflicted by the plague, he grew more and more remote, and she knew she must not cast a backwards glance towards that immoderate thing that went its own way alone and without remorse, it was an entire world, a small, very small world shrunken up by doubt, by continual inspection, it was immoderate but small, and the most important thing was to keep it from turning back towards you; perhaps the coldest glaciers were more sensitive than she'd thought, they lived their own autonomous life in changing atmospheres; when she got up in the morning she was preoccupied with the mountain, with its sky and air, and though it was a shame that they discharged the busloads of tourists and all that they brought in their wake too close to the snow-capped summits, the breath that wafted down from the heights was pure and fresh, she could imagine all the good it did, she wondered what kind of trees she could see in the distance, struggling against the austerity of the rocks; every species on earth learned the art of cohabitation, of living with others, every species except man, but why and what was she doing in that savage scenery — nothing, living, wandering, wandering, like so many others who, like herself, refused to admit it; she made her way towards the holy mountain, towards a dream which would illuminate her though only in an interior way, rather than towards those picturesque hills and valleys that her eyes reflected without seeing, for the mountain was the cure, oblivion, annihilation in the space of this world she had left behind, of this world of love that had punished her — or rather, the truth was that she'd had the sagacity to deprive herself of it in order to avoid yet sharper pain — and at the moment when she thought she finally couldn't remember him any more, he appeared, looming in all the others who still expressed his thirst for life, for love, in his stead; there had been the joyous couple of skaters and then, during her trip to Switzerland, she had suddenly seen two mountain-climbers studying a map just outside a tiny village, devouring with their eyes the names of mountains that seemed extremely well suited to their nordic appetites, "*Wetterhorn*", "*Mettenberg*", "*Finsteraarhorn*", the two girls murmured, hugging each other in delight at their exploration of the world; it gave Florence a start to see them so close in this circle of just-born ecstasy that had lodged itself between two beings from whom she couldn't part, "*Wetterhorn*", *Mettenberg*", she could imagine the shared ascension, the shared exhaustion, the reddened cheeks and dishevelled hair; the skaters had been only children, but these two were about thirty, Florence thought, they belonged to a wilful, conscious generation that made her seem insignificant; she had so little courage, while the mountain climbers feared nothing, neither man's judgement nor the mountain they already dominated with their frank gaze; who were they, what goal did they have in mind as they undertook, together, this pilgrimage towards the future; the mountain watched, it listened to everything that came and went around it, its haze swallowed up all visitors, confident or sad, swallowed their touching stories and their daring and drew each one's silence to rest against its flanks; maybe the two girls would decide to pitch their tent up there, where the air was always cool, and Florence would forget them, would never see them again, living two by two, red cheeks, rumpled hair, losing yourself with another person in some cold, wooded lair—Florence had to forget all that, for such things could no longer be counted among her familiar privileges in this world, not for a long time to come. The mountain killed, usurped those graceful lives, life destroyed life, the village dozed off around nine o'clock at night, anaesthetized by a purple vapour that was some-

times icy cold, sometimes heavy and warm, and everything fell into silence: the village and Florence alike were
suspended on the glacier's silence, on its snows; but not
even that serenity, that contentment, when she possessed
it, could appease her terror; one could hear the
mountain-climbers' footsteps as they descended in the
calm of evening and suddenly everyone was hastening
towards evening because the day had weighed on each of
them in his own fashion, thought Florence, and now the
heaviness of this still time was going to be jostled, agitated,
it was the life of labour driving off the other life, the life of
silence, the silence one had probably imposed in spite of
oneself; sometimes a storm broke suddenly, as if to accompany this bustling activity, and at such moments what
wind of anguish must have gone blowing along the wind-
ing mountain roads and through anyone who had gone
astray in the great folds of snow, thought Florence, it
seemed to be forbidden to conquer the mountain's beauty,
its whiteness, its blinding luminosity; all you really knew
about nature, thought Florence, was that it would be there
tomorrow to outlive you and to watch you die; the storm
drove those who had been relaxing on the café terraces
inside, towards warmth and shadows, and the apocalypse
passed, it took but an instant, you found yourself drenched
and chilled, the drunkenness had passed — or did the
valley's dry wind affect only those who were down below,
sheltered, the tables that had been part of the afternoon
festivities that told of their gluttony and their boundless
leisure, crumpled up under the rumbling storms; how
feeble our happiness was, how quickly it yielded before
foreign dictatorships such as cold, wind, rain; the bees and

the birds had fled, a driving rain was falling, maybe it would even snow, the white summits remained unalterable; bees, birds, people were just particles of dust, the house the only shelter, someone said, "It's so warm here, you'd think they'd turned the heat on," the sky cleared shortly, leaving them indifferent because the house, the roof had comforted them, life went on and that evening you kept the night to come for yourself, the night that the person you might have preserved near yourself, for yourself, wouldn't share; Florence could no longer bear the presence of all those complacent, enticing couples but they crowded around you in spite of yourself, you had to choose between living and eating with them or ceasing to exist, you were supposed to live in twosomes, taking pains to avoid the deathly solitude that pursued you all through your life; Florence, who only the day before had been seen with her husband, now became an awkward creature for the first time in that lonely retreat, her presence a source of embarrassment or, in the case of more benevolent observers, a source of pity — pity, for Florence who abhorred pity and degradation in any form; and yet as her entire being settled into this novel hardness towards men, so like the hardness of the glaciers, she realized that if she had been indifferent to women, to their lives, to their particular destiny in this world for such a long time, it was because until then she'd only had eyes for her husband and had lived with him alone, for him alone, while all the rest had gone on without her, without them, all the rest had been caught up in the movement of the blind crowd, but now she had to admit that the blindest of all was not that human mass whose hardships she'd never perceived before that day, but she herself: for a very, very long time she had thought and lived only for him, for his joys and pleasures, thus for herself above all, for the savour of a life whose future she preferred to ignore; it shamed her to think that others had long since preceded her in that struggle and that questioning of their destinies while she lived in idleness, in a guilty mental indifference which would now exact its price in the sufferings of her body; it was a dreadful debt, for it may be impossible, she thought, to avoid that which fate expects from us; formerly her gestures had been rich with subtleties and voluptuous sonorities that spoke to her alone, that precipitated her immediately into distracted reflections from which every-one else was excluded; so she had barely taken notice of those women they had met one day, a long time ago since it was when her husband still loved her and they had visited the ruins of an abbey together, it was in England, they loved each other, they were always together, maybe it was before the birth of their son, they had shared infinite hopes between themselves, she hadn't yet known fear, they'd applied such arrogance to living in those already long-gone days; they had been together when they had come across the two women in the abbey, and yet she alone remembered them for the women, who had sur-vived in some abstract zone of her mind for so long, now surfaced to assert the drama of life she had so long pretended to ignore; her vision of the abbey and the surrounding meadows, even the stormy sky that flooded the clefts of the stones with brilliance when it momentar-ily cleared — everything she had seen and felt in that place that had once been inhabited by prayer was linked to the two women, to the drama that she had understood at a glimpse and immediately forgotten for the sake of her own comfort; because of that couple the abbey told a story that was no longer sacred but profane: it told of the need to live your own life; unlike that of the mountain-climbers or the skaters, this scene had contained no action; one of the women might have been fifty or so, the other was younger, both had children they'd brought along for a walk in the green fields, but the rain had prevented the walk and now the children were waiting for their mothers in the car, bickering among themselves while their mothers walked along the worn archways of the abbey, each one doing her best, by means of a calm but painful conversation broken up by whispers and inhibited silences, to convert their painfully separate lives into a future consolation, the "couple"; the word "decision" haunted their reticent, alarmed voices, they were pressed and battered by the urgency of a union that overwhelmed them, of which they spoke only with discretion and prudence, but there in the abbey their decision might become reality, certainty, or outright disaster, and the stormy sky and its clouds came and went above them, in that clearing in which their lives were suspended, their husbands at home, their children in the car, all these scenes whirled around them and the vertigo of their thoughts, they who were separated, would they finally be able to come to each other without lying, would their children belong to one family or would they be wrested from them; the word "couple" contained all that, what had become of them, Florence wondered, she would never know; the wrenching pain and power of that simple word "couple" — especially wrenching when you are on the outside, but for a long time it was the others who were on the outside, the others who envied the peace, the nest, the warmth you had found — was linked too in Florence's mind to the memory of a woman, it was in England again during those privileged hours when she and her husband were still satisfied with each other; they had finished their dinner but were dallying over a bottle of one of the excellent wines they were fond of, watching the families leaving their tables like well-trained flocks, leaving the soiled and stained tablecloths that had been so white a short time before; vacation time signified a return to games between children and parents in the evening — trying for all concerned but one hastened towards them at sunset as if finally to bring the day to a close, thought Florence, and suddenly she'd felt a rambling presence close by, a big girl who didn't know what to do with her ungainly body, she was smoking a cigarette as she tagged along after the line of children she was minding, a governess or a maid, very young, and just as preoccupied with herself as the two women of the abbey had been, maybe she'd been hired for the summer but this role that seemed to overwhelm her was obviously not really hers, who am I, she seemed to ask Florence, slowing her pace as she neared her, is this what my life is, living among them, their parents don't respect me, the maid, the governess, no, take me away from all of them; she was smoking a cigarette, she didn't say anything, she was attracted by Florence without even realizing it, she had noticed Florence's straight back, the proud nape of her neck, and she found in her a kind of stability, a nobility in living that she admired without understanding, and yet it wasn't the couple Florence formed with her husband that attracted her for she hadn't even taken notice of his existence, what she admired was Florence, and the stiff truth she seemed to possess, even if it was only a potential Florence herself put to no use; she had understood or felt who Florence was and what kind of being she might one day become without him, maybe that was what had stirred Florence to fear and repulsion for the young English girl, she met her often and couldn't run away from her, like Judith Lange who would come a lot later she knew too much about her, and yet it pleased her to catch this fresh, sensitive character in moments of emotion, much as it would have pleased her to follow the metamorphoses of a painting in changing lights, but she would have liked to be invisible and compact for the girl, instead of the fragmented creature suffering from a secret wound that the young English girl had perceived, something that could be separated from him, didn't it expose Florence completely? — she fled, the portent of this skeleton of solitude frightened her, and the young governess, moved by an instinct of solidarity, felt it all, felt it for herself as well as for Florence, she didn't know how to speak to her; in Florence's case, surprising the character of her painting in all her awkwardness was a cruel, facile exercise — the young English girl had to take part in the games the children played on the beach, she came in with them in the evening, her jet-black hair smoothed by the sea-water and sticking to her handsome, austere forehead, they scolded her because of a sick child, they corrected her manners, and Florence was there — before that beautiful, inclined, blushing forehead — in the dim shadows of the corridor she saw her when evening came, putting a baby to sleep, rocking him almost as though she were rocking herself so ill-suited to these tasks did she seem in her thick Irish sweater and her grey woollen socks, with her boyish mien, so that the maternal duties imposed on her seemed all the more laughable because she carried them out with such complete sincerity, she was a fine being who had been shut up there by chance and who aspired to break out of her prison; and Florence, with her coldness and her false determination, represented freedom for her, and also the freedom money can bring — for it was the obligation to earn her living according to terms that were not of her own choosing and that she hadn't accepted that was such a burden to her; she was a captive of that obligation, on her island, while Florence was a free woman for although she had bound her existence to a man she remained, behind that façade of appearances, a free woman — that was what had spontaneously drawn the young English girl to her and she would have liked to take off with her, to cross the boundaries that kept her real life at a distance; and it dawned on Florence now that she could be terribly disappointing for others, the young governess for example, she had let her down just as she let all the others down by not living up to what she seemed to promise, she offered nothing, for her egoism held back all she could have given, she sometimes imagined she was stingy but she was blighted with a defect far worse than stinginess, she thought; she felt, and it was a feeling akin to terror, that if she offered all that her physical appearance led one to expect of her, her moral being might simply dissolve, melt away to nothingness: none of them realized that she was only made of pieces, scattered fragments whose assembly or order was beyond her imagination; her silence veiled nothing but cries and chaos, and when the young governess had passed her nonchalantly, a cigarette in her hand, she had upset this silent tumult, loosened the knot of fright, as would Judith Lange later on; it was late in Florence's life and not only had she continued to disappoint others, she thought — with the vision before her of the young governess surrounded by spoiled children who had no respect for life, children who might grow up to be men or monsters — but she in turn had also been disappointed, and although she would have gone on disappointing others, she would have understood now, so late in the day, the young governess' call, maybe she would even have found the words that bring relief and liberation, which was what people expected of her when they saw her; but perhaps that was merely an illusion, for Mike was close by, rocking his own pain while he rocked his sister Jojo, and she made no move to console him, she looked at him without seeing him, mute and sterile in her compassion, a slave to the evil that was in her and not in him for it wasn't possible to leave one's body to suffer in that of another person — the way human beings were made they only reached out towards another body in search of pleasure, not pain — and yet Florence was revolted by the memory of her former indifference, she could have cried when she thought of the two women in the abbey and of the governess, as she could have cried for herself perhaps, or for the sympathy and understanding that each of those women stirred in her for the fragments of herself lost in time, the fragments she had never managed to put together, to polish up, because of her lack of courage or will-power; and also, when she projected her image onto the destiny of women whose paths had crossed hers, she projected herself "alive" and not dead, she had a future, for the others with their projects and their tenacity were part of an active universe, they permitted her to forget about her agony and the shameful weakness that isolated her here with Mike and Gloria in this circle of terror where death germinated, where death was ready and waiting; in turn she became the skaters, the mountain-climbers, above all she became those hesitant forms on the verge of a capital decision, the women in the abbey and the young governess with the jet-black hair, all those lives belonged to her, and near them, with them, she would have liked to make a final attempt at that total failure called "living"; Florence had also seen couples of survivors among those she'd observed, couples united by invisibly spilled blood, and perhaps the strongest, most intricate ties were those formed when time united someone who had formerly been counted among the victims with a partner who had stood with the executioners, or the occasional, mysterious marriage of two victims who were bound to each other for life by a similar humiliation, all these different kinds of couples existed, co-existed, and their obscure past was often barely perceptible under the pleasure-seeking mask of the present; thus Florence, who had brushed aside those pedantic families who had welcomed so poorly the young governess and her hopes, liked, on the contrary, to link her solitude to those couples gifted for survival and the miracle of charity or simple, heartfelt decency in which she no longer believed; she spoke little but she listened, silently respectful of these

temples of discovery which she came across so rarely; it
was nice to think that while the young governess' melancholy watches over the rough children at last drew to a
close — for they would eventually be sent off to bed and
she would finally be free to go down to the beach alone —
the German couple would disappear, and their disappearance was for Florence a symbolic moment, a reminder that
life could branch out in other ways and that despite the
crumbling brought on by tragedy you could go on living
and marvelling at life; they were a young couple but they
seemed ageless compared to others; their two adopted
children had survived the massacres in Indochina and they
all shared, with their complex, troubled pasts, a tacit
harmony in the present, with the present, against the
troubles of the past, and the elegance of this silent pact was
confirmed in Florence's mind by the fact that she didn't
feel rejected in their company in spite of their propensity
for happiness; they accepted her like another of those
enigmas of misfortune they had known but never mentioned, she was there among them like a witness who
might learn to survive one day, but nobody demanded it of
her as a duty, it was just a passing breath, a pacific warning
that seemed to say, "There's life, there's death, you can
still choose the one you prefer," and then it seemed to her
that her combat wouldn't necessarily be a fatal one, or
rather that the crouching, silent executioner she carried in
her, the executioner that the couple of survivors had
looked in the eye and had braved, wouldn't come stealthily to vanquish her. Florence would have liked to tell
Judith Lange, who saw the stigmata of the past everywhere, that the passing of generations taught survival to

the dead and was a lesson in well-being that often drove off the ghost of ancient misfortunes; a lot of survivors had told her so, without words or tears; if you were unhappy with yourself, in your own home, with your own race, you could always create new families, unless, like Florence, you were inhabited by egoism and a craving for nothingness; but she was there, she had taken the first step, she was there between Mike and Gloria, she was no longer shut up in her home, in herself, and this transformed her past into a gaping, painful thing because she no longer inhabited it; the German couple of today with their Asian children, the Japanese youths of today that she came across everywhere — these signified the passing of the generations and revealed a new coherence in the duties of the present; didn't it take heroic courage or indifference to face up to a present that promised so little peace, that was still hazy with blood, and didn't you even have to forget that Hiroshima had left its cancerous seed in you, in your mother, in your descendants, for man's most admirable quality, thought Florence, was his capacity to survive in spite of all the murderous atrocities that he had fathered, and in time, if you survived, you dominated the world's apathy, you pursued the search in darkness, against death itself, and the taste of nothingness was replaced by a curiosity she no longer felt, this feeling of curiosity was apparently unalterable, for those who felt it survived everything and made life on earth durable and concrete for themselves as well as for others, they took root and settled on earth just when she was getting ready to leave it; following the living and the survivors, with the knowledge that she would never see them again, gave her a strange sensation; she was well aware that she was going to drift and wander alone towards her place of torment although she knew her husband wasn't worth that much passivity or this total rupture with the world, he didn't deserve any of it, but certain people preferred to decide their supreme condemnation by themselves, and those who had never had a will to live, she thought, especially the will to go on living when they were abandoned, thought they justified themselves by the sole act of will they accomplished in dying, all their courage rose to burn itself out in the throbbing pain of lucidity and consciousness; in Florence's case, that lucidity had taken control of the details and mechanisms of a passion that could destroy her; indirectly her husband was her executioner since life had begun to steal softly, stealthily from her when he'd left her, and now she told herself that if she hadn't responded to the young governess' spontaneity, nor later on to Judith Lange's pure, redeeming tenderness, it was because such joys of life were no longer meant for her, they had been stripped from her while her husband caressed her hand, inflicting all his boredom, his nostalgia for something else, upon her; already, already she had become an intruder in this world, little by little she had become a stray ghost and the moment would arrive when she was nothing, not even an absurd human form in Mike's and Gloria's eyes, in the eyes of those who kept up their unknowing vigil over her when she was convinced she was the sole guardian of her body; she had believed that by leaving him, by leaving everything, she would find a new breath of life in herself and suddenly, just when she'd noticed that all those who surrounded her were at home in the world — even when they were suspended between two horizons, at the foot of the mountain, against the ridge of the glacier, they were at home everywhere since they went on living, preferably in twosomes or in larger groups, they bundled themselves up in the human layers she was fleeing, sank down into cold, eternal nature by twos or in groups — at that instant she'd felt how her body was detaching itself from her, she saw them all for the last time but she wasn't there and nature's splendours could no longer bring her consolation, for you lived and loved in a dream and when you woke up it was already over; was it not a dream to believe in these deceitful worldly realities, to actually cling to them in vain? Certain images sharpened the sense of annihilation and dissolution of her physical being; the snickering clamour of a group of high school students who came towards her without seeing her during a stop in a train station, it was a masquerade day and they were noisy, but their funereal masks, their black and white striped costumes, and above all the way they ran towards the invisible point she was to them, all appeared to her as the unleashing of ill-omens against her, pointing out that death was really coming to meet her, or at least to meet her body which no one noticed any more, not even during a brief stop for refreshments in a train station; from then on there was a strangeness about her, in her, which was why the students had encroached upon her space, had peopled her terror with their joyful cries — or had she imagined it? She also recalled, among the images that had dispossessed her, the moment during a mountain hike in which she had suddenly felt that those who were with her were taking flight or disintegrating in a cold, incandescent fog; whether they went on foot or took the funicular railway, each of them seemed to embark upon a personal exodus, heading for a dangerous dead-end at the heart of infinity, and all of them would return from these deep, silent territories except her; they continued their joyful climbs and descents, their open souls full of gratitude towards their creator, while she felt nothing but fright, saw nothing but the cold, glowing fog before her, heard its whip descending from the summits of silence and hail to flay her bones. We'll be in the desert, thought Mike, a long way from here, from all of them, the indigo bush that cures, the desert lavender and honey, he murmured to Jojo while stroking her hair, and Florence saw Mike's long pale hand resting on his sister's head, the hand, innocent and teasing as it toyed with the curly hair, seemed to hold so many tangible promises, so many promises that life would not fulfil because of the curse that hovered there in the room, over Mike, ready to blast him; Florence wondered if, like herself, Mike had begun to leave his body, she wondered into what cold, glowing fog he felt it sliding, unable to control the thing that slipped away like that, mutely, mutely, but he'd pinched his lips and said nothing, said nothing, for his pain matured in silence, he let Jojo's soft hair slide between his fingers and he gazed off into the distance; when had he had that dream, when had he woken up crying on Luigi's hard shoulder — his brother had pushed him off in disgust, him and his obscure misfortune that shared a bed with innocence, Luigi's peculiar innocence in life, his robust health — in the dream Mike had been sent off, far away, to an island where he had to crush stones all day beneath a white, torrid sun, bent over by the slavish labour he crawled in the dust, he was thirsty, he could feel the eyes of all his executioners against his broken back, men in white, he couldn't see their faces, maybe they didn't have any, by their obscure, terrifying actions they were plotting against him and he couldn't escape, they stood there like a rampart, like a deadly cliff, and Mike had to yield to their blind power without understanding it and then suddenly he recognized her in the distance, it was she, Judith Lange, she was coming, alone, to get him, in a sumptuous sailboat that glided softly over the placid water; she waved to him, he would soon be at her side and she would save him from the islanders' relentless slavery, she would take him back with her, but the dream was rapidly blotted out by another which was even more disturbing because Mike in his tormented sleep attained perhaps the peak of that consciousness which determines even the batting of our eyelids in slumber, that point which Florence lucidly identified when she wasn't dreaming as the first separation of the soul and the body that occurs at the beginning of the death-agony, for just as Florence had been able to watch her body dissolve in the haze of the train station the day she had seen the masked adolescents, and had experienced the sensation of losing herself indistinctly among the others in the furrows of snow and fog high up on the mountain, so Mike had departed from his body locked in on all sides by suffering, he had flown over its shape, coming and going inside that physical entity he had stripped himself of; and not being there any more, no longer being engulfed, confined to silence and secrecy in the spirals of muscular and nervous fibres that had restrained him for so long, gave him a wonderful sensation of deliverance, after being compressed by that shivering anatomy for such a long time, suffocated in its vital, luminous nerve fibres, he was suddenly free; but it was a dream and he woke up crying, for none of it was true, you woke up in the same old place, lacerated in the arched body that had left you for a moment, for the fleeting moment of consciousness between life and death, and the body was so slow to die for God never blessed it with oblivion; on the contrary, that pitiless flame of consciousness was stoked to the very end and the body burned so readily under the cold torture, thought Florence, that one might have thought that consciousness made it immortal; yes, thought Florence, all these tangible promises that take the form of our hands, of our fingers, these promises that we betray, and she saw Frédérike again as she'd been sitting beside her on the stairs a few minutes earlier, speaking to her of Mozart's *Requiem*, once again she saw the young governess putting the cigarette to her lips, expecting Florence to offer her promises and joys of life that Florence had always been careful never to offer or satisfy for she was of those who don't give of themselves, she'd given herself just once, and to one single man, but it already seemed as if that had happened in another life and now that life glided past her like a series of paintings; some of them were very energetic and full of life, like the wild apparition of a shepherd who had emerged from the bushes and given her a bemused smile when she'd thought she was alone and far removed from everything, and she'd paused before him and had returned his smile before resuming her silent ascent with a heavy foot; he'd followed her with his eyes, he'd watched her fade away into darkness, she thought, then he had forgotten her, but the boy had seemed so alive that the countryside she'd been seeing in terms of death and stagnation was suddenly buoyed up by a secret resurrection, a hope, an entire field of yellow flowers had appeared before her eyes at the same time as the shepherd, and suddenly energetic labour seemed something beautiful in that setting; and other paintings, her reward, were close by, now devoid of the sensual rumbling that had characterized them in life and deprived of the awareness of the present that had once illuminated them, they came to Florence's mind like wrecks, in these paintings she and her husband were still a couple, even the weariness of their bodies was intertwined, indissoluble; and her husband's caress throbbing in her entire body, the taste of those indissoluble instants, of those feverish unions that still resounded in her, of this entangling of their skins and blood from which she could no longer escape, not even on the threshold of death, sharpened her longing for nothingness and peace, for the nothingness that would be an antidote to pleasure and amorous languor, an antidote above all to the confusion of their two essences which she wanted to end; perhaps that was what took so long to die out between them, the sensuality of their brown bodies at rest; even if she was no longer there in the warmth of his embrace, the things that had surrounded them remained, even a mere spot on a wall had eternal repercussions here — a spot on the wall, a wall, the size of a bed, curtains rustling in the wind — they immediately evoked scenes of a long-lasting enchantment, and now her wounded soul capitulated unwillingly before them: she and her husband had known only fleeting moments of happiness in those surroundings, there where they had sought an idyll they had often fallen to quarrelling, they had avoided the pitfalls of meaningful language, straying instead into banalities that proved to be their downfall, for this evil that they were avoiding naming and that was right there all along rose up suddenly before them, so devastatingly if silently present in all the pretexts they resorted to that they looked at each other with consternation and seemed utterly dismayed; where did this misunderstanding, this unsettling of all their emotions, come from, how had it rooted itself between them when everything seemed to have begun so calmly with a simple discussion, perhaps about a horse race or some other subject that aroused their competitive instincts; suddenly the indissoluble bond was threatened, tomorrow it might be severed, dead, destroyed, they had trembled with fear but they hadn't said anything, they were weary and their brown bodies were still intertwined in the dawn light but it was no longer he, it was no longer she, from that point on they were strangers, they didn't move any more, didn't sweat, they weren't living, dust was going to settle and cover them in their ecstatic paralysis, their lethargy, it was all going to disappear, fade away, or else be eaten by worms, yes, thought Florence, nothingness was going to annihilate them forever, and she would feel such joy once she was far from their voices and complaints — or would she always see them as she saw them, the two of them, now; he and she might be strangers but they were her strangers, she recognized both their gaits, their footsteps, their breaths, she recognized the wetness of their eyes even if it no longer moved her, she knew exactly how they behaved towards each other after a night of drunkenness, a night of love, or a night of hate, she knew the weariness of each of their faces and she had known, in both of them, their particular form of pride, shame, modesty, and haughtiness, as she knew every detail of the exasperated truce that followed a demonstration of these emotions; sometimes she considered the couple they had formed with irony and pity: they too had been deceived and deluded, and she recalled a night of celebration in which they'd had the illusion, in their drunkenness, of sleeping in a first-class hotel near the sea only to wake up in the morning in a sordid room beside a slaughterhouse, and thus their dream instead of ending joyously terminated in a bloody vapour, in the smell of death that everywhere reminds us of our crimes; and until today she had forgotten that whirlwind of cries and blood for they had been quick to drown their disillusions in champagne and love, or else to flee, and yet in those days the presence of the slaughterhouse hadn't disturbed her, maybe she had even been convinced that they both needed a dose of abasement to really live, that it was a luxury, one of love's fantasies; and now the only humiliation that tormented her was the thoughtlessness of the two lovers who had given themselves over to the joys of life while a silent death had lain in wait for them, death had been present, she thought, in each of their abandonments, they had never been aware of its breath passing over their cheeks, they hadn't moved, hadn't spoken, hadn't run away, it had shut itself up in their house with them, it had slipped between the sheets with them and had drunk up all the warmth and fragrance of the fine summer in bloom at the window; it had liked to see them defenceless among their furniture and their paintings, supple and naked, they belonged to it, they would fade out each into the other and death would take them in one single kiss, long and soft, the transparency of love had already drawn them closer to it, they had only to remain as they were, united and rigid, they wouldn't see it coming; a few days had passed since they had gone out and they had even forgotten they were hungry, death liked such prey, gullible, transparent, stretched out in big beds, and this slow drawing out of two apparently extinct, drowsy lives carried death's signature; who would have thought, anyway, that they were alive and breathing for even the fabric of their clothes slept lewdly on a chair, having stolen its pale, transparent lustre from them; and while the golden, endless summer bloomed at the window, warming them with its light and fire, they didn't know, no, at that point they didn't know that death was there close by, stubbornly drinking up all the warmth. No, the cat wouldn't go back under the bridges, he wouldn't even go near the lair in which Gabrielle Dubois, the waitress, lived with dignity, and he would soon part ways with Berthe Agneli for he sensed that the unfortunate girl no longer needed him; instead of making for the city's rubble, he would go off towards the good neighbourhoods where he would dream and bask in the sun, alone at long last; Berthe Agneli obstinately clutched her books to her chest, she didn't like anyone, she chased the cat off with her foot and he had pity on her gruffness, she was always bumping into things when she walked, she was probably a bit cold, a shame when it was so nice out, she went into a university café and the cat went off alone, dirty and muddy as he was, feeling great satisfaction at being alive — the frost gardens in the distance were beginning to thaw, there were feasts of birds in the country, escape was right there, it was irresistible; and now he headed towards other summer greenery, his heart throbbing, his head held high, but what would become of Berthe Agneli, what would become of her tomorrow and later on, Berthe opened a book on her lap and avidly set to reading the pages covered with incomprehensible signs, and suddenly her eyes dimmed with tears for she was absolutely convinced of her failure in life, failure was inscribed in her, they all felt it, especially her professors who wondered what that haggard, that silent but haggard creature was doing in their midst, the daughter of a man who had killed, she carried in her the misery of those lives the paternal hand had torn to shreds, cut short; maybe, yes, as time went by maybe they'd give Mike a bit of liquid morphine, you had to lull consciousness to sleep, rock it like a child; perhaps her existence, perhaps Berthe Angeli's life would be just as brief, just as fluctuating and precarious as the life of the stray cat that had followed her, and she gazed off into the distance, towards the sunny street, probing the fuzzy, undulating, terror-filled future which the others didn't perceive, laughing and having fun outside, Lucia — my little sister — no, she'd never see her again; two Christians were speaking close by, she saw them from the back, students her age, and one of them, whose name was Jean-François, was saying to his friend, "I saw the celestial Jerusalem"; Berthe listened to their incomprehensible language, celestial Jerusalem, the words had been pronounced calmly in a rational tone, the

sounds whipped Berthe Agneli's soul, what right did they
have, what right, she hid her face in her hands, her eyes
were dry now, "A voice," the student continued, "a voice
told me to go back to the earth"; absorbed as they were in
their theological appeasement, they ignored the hate that
burned in her heart, there's no celestial Jerusalem, said
Berthe Agneli, hell is right here, near you, but she hadn't
said anything and they went on talking, their monotonous
voices no longer reached her, maybe she would start
coming here regularly to read and study, her eyes were
dry, she was no longer afraid, her hands no longer shook,
and Lucia said to John, we'll live in the streets, at home
there was Gloria and later Charlie who'd be released from
prison one day, he might rape her, Gloria said, there were
Mike and Jojo, they all knew she wouldn't come back,
John went up and down the steps of a grocery store, it was
his way of waiting for clients, John's eyes were empty like
Dmitri's, Lucia waited in the street, contemplating the
frayed hem of her jeans, the sky was blue, push this
emptiness back to the very limits of eternity, John, Dmitri,
and the others, she wasn't thinking about anything, wasn't
thinking of Mike or Gloria, she looked at the sky, there
was so much tranquillity, so much indifference in that blue
sky, just remember you're not alone in the world, Gabrielle Dubois had told her, I've got a lair under the
Jacques-Cartier Bridge, I feed those who are hungry, and
the cat said to himself, I won't go that way, it would be my
ruin, in spring and summer huge, greedy rats emerge from
all sides, slimy and stinking, but the rat isn't always
harmful, the rat shared the cat's frenetic love of life, he was
a survivor, a frenetic survivor, and for that very reason he

deserved praise, his presence in this world was just as fraudulent as ours, one respected it; a bit farther up there was a path of lilacs and a cool yard where a few boys, stripped to the waist, were playing ball, the cat was wary of dark yards and hooligans but no enemy seemed to be present in this place, light abounded everywhere, he came and went with a proud, malicious eye, and the boys jumped up and down, a laughing voice said, let's catch him, let's, let's, the perverse words pierced him, pierced the innocence of his frightened heart, what a catastrophe, he thought, on such a nice day with such warm light, but dirty and muddy as he was, with his coat in tatters, he felt great satisfaction at being alive; the Bach cantata was almost finished, Madame Langenais' daughters were studying in their rooms, you could hardly hear them moving and living in them, but the family din would take up again at supper time, and then it would be evening, Madame Langenais always felt fear at its approach now that her daughters went out at night, but fortunately the light had been dying more slowly for the past few days, the days were growing longer, but why these feminist meetings in the evening, already, what were they lacking, the volume of Tolstoy was resting on the table near the fireplace, she devoted such fine hours to music and reading, but they were hours already gone, thought Josephine, rubbing her hands, for her husband would be home soon; tomorrow I'll listen to the *Art of the Fugue*, how am I going to break the news to Charles, selling the house, the sabbatical year; during dinner, or maybe later, late in the evening, once we're alone in front of the fire, I'll remind him of the French woman's story, the way her baby came down with whooping cough during the exodus, I'll say to him, listen, Charles, I haven't really lived at all yet; Madame Langenais paced up and down, meditating in her house with the blue drapes, the past might totter, but the thought of the future infused her with a happiness she'd never known, and she had just decided that she'd go to Vienna, alone or with Charles, when she heard her husband's step in the hall, "I had a little mishap with my glasses," he explained to his wife, pointing to his tired face, and contrary to habit he retreated to his study without even kissing Josephine; all that fuss for a pair of glasses, thought Madame Langenais, men are so fragile, the girls were silent in their rooms, the Bach cantata was almost finished, I never did like the size of this place, thought Madame Langenais, that's how I'll broach the subject with Charles tonight, the exodus, the baby with the whooping cough; and then there was a brusque torment, Judith's voice saying in her ear, "Josephine, I love you, in spite of everything, Josephine, you'll do great things"; no, Micheline, Gisèle, and Marianne mustn't turn out like her, the tip of Gilbert's cap was coming and going at the window, "Josephine, I love you in spite of everything," it was a raucous, insinuating, loving voice, the voice of this child who'd always piqued and irritated her; Madame Langenais opened the livingroom window and asked Gilbert to join her for tea but Gilbert didn't understand, he'd never been invited into the house, he spoke of his rosebushes, of mice that would have to be exterminated, of the abandoned state of gardens in winter, of the subtle ways in which nature suffered during that season; Madame Langenais listened to him, gazing off into the distance; the days were long now, from her flowery mountain Josephine contemplated the city and the flood of light that gradually shaded off below. "The feeling of fright is attenuated at the end of the work," Frédérike had said, sitting close to her on the stairs, "for Mozart saw death as a friend," but none of that is true, thought Florence, we need to carry one final consolation off into nothingness with us, even if it's false, maybe this courage, this capacity to reassure ourselves, is expected of us... suddenly, the greatest consolation of all was having all these people there with her, Mike, Gloria, people who although she didn't know them and didn't speak to them had offered her this last scene of her life, they, with their misfortunes and their joys, had brought her such peace of mind that during all this time — a whole day, maybe — she had forgotten that she had come there to die; they hadn't lied to her, they hadn't betrayed her, they had placed themselves between her and the forbidden threshold to envelop and distract her, they were like the works of art she'd admired in museums in former days but at the time she'd ignored the tragic aspect of existence that bound the work of art and life together, rendered them inseparable; and this was so true that the Sick Child, as depicted by Munch, was not elsewhere, in some barren eternity, but here, just a few feet away from Florence, it was right here among them that he endured his protracted, obsessive eternity, like a work of art enclosed in its own silence, he spoke little, he seemed to be deaf to everything, for this endless cry of revolt had to be retained in oneself, this cry that could no longer be silenced, it went on night and day, it would never die out; what would become of us if all these cries should escape? Art was so very real that Florence, who just the day before had been barely human, now found herself enclosed in Munch's *Agony* with a cold, glowing fog descending upon her, and close by, in the red and black light, the light of the night that would soon fall, a few figures still leaned over towards her, perhaps these figures would eventually become, who knows, just as distracted and vague as the lonely human figures she'd followed and watched disappear in the mountain fog a long time ago; she recalled that a frothy fog had come down from the Kleine Scheidegg glaciers, and suddenly the shrill call of a bagpipe had attracted the motionless traveller to the invisible peaks and he had strayed off in ecstasy towards that voice that came from the sky; maybe the end of the odyssey was just this, harkening to the voice, letting yourself be swallowed up by invisible powers that petrified you until you faded away into nothingness. It's strange, thought Gabrielle Dubois as she went along her street, it's strange that the old alley-cat no longer comes around here, when spring arrives you're supposed to wash your curtains, scrub everything clean, you never know when somebody might come, a clean tablecloth, flowers in a bowl, she would wait, sitting by the window, it was going to be a hot summer, cars slid silently by on the bridge, the bridge and its iridescent nights, all this life so close around her, around this heart of hers that was like a desert, she had tended the victorious wounds of the brave tom-cat but we're not always the victors, and as for Lucia, maybe it wasn't too late to persuade her to go back to school, the florist had told her the flowers came from Holland, they needed water, they were going to wilt,

Gabrielle Dubois ran, ran with small, contained bounds towards her lair, and Gloria said to Mike, shaking him hard, did you hear that awful noise upstairs, no Mike hadn't heard anything, there was fear in his eyes but he hadn't heard anything, he said, it seemed to Florence herself that the gun had gone off with a muffled sound, the explosion took place inside, she told herself, that way she wouldn't have time to suffer, suddenly she had the vision of an unexpected scene, she thought she'd forgotten it, while she wandered, wandered among people one Christmas Eve she had exchanged a few words with a black man who held his little girl on his knees, it was a stormy night and the man, the little girl, and Florence were spending Christmas Eve together, wandering, they were in an airport waiting for the storm to let up and she was surprised to see them again now; so the face of her passion had left her at long last and her last moments were haunted by the face of a stranger, of a wanderer like herself, the exact spot, her husband had said, is here, right next to the heart, she didn't moan, her blood spilled out noiselessly, dully, she hadn't called them but someone opened the door, they were there, Mike, Gloria, Frédér-ike, Gloria said to Mike, quick, call an ambulance, but he looked at Florence without moving, he was standing against the door, his face extremely pale beneath the white bandage that girded his head, soon she would no longer see them, she would no longer see Mike, his handsome face was going to dissolve in the cold, glowing fog, Mike said to Gloria, look, Mom, she's come, Judith Lange, she comes every day at this time, and perhaps it was true, or was it the sudden apparition of a final hope, Judith Lange approached the bed and bent over her saying, "Come back, come back to earth with me," but it was just a silhouette in the fog, just a ghost, maybe, she no longer saw them, she had closed her eyes.